The Girl
In The
Attic

JOY WODHAMS

DEDICATION

To my daughter Lindsay and to friends Tracey, Dot and
Angela who patiently previewed this book for me.

One

I read a book once. The Count of Monte Cristo. Or was it *The Man in the Iron Mask?* I can't be sure, it was such a long, long time ago. But in this book - or some other book - a man had been imprisoned, all alone, for years and years and years, and he marked the days by scratching on the walls of his cell. Seven days for the week. Fifty two weeks for the year. On and on and on.

I wish I'd thought to do that. It's too late now. All I know are the days and the nights. The sun comes up, the sun goes down. Sometimes it rains. Sometimes there are storms and the rain thuds heavily on the roof and I see lightning in the sky. Sometimes mist from the sea creeps in through the cracks around the window and I sniff it eagerly.

But I don't know how many days or weeks or years I've been here. Time means nothing when there are no events to mark it.

Josh knelt up on the bench and flattened his nose against the window.

'Look! There's the sea!'

They had left the A303 and the huge Hymer camper van was inching its way along narrow lanes, down into a valley one minute, on top of the world the next, with the deep blue sea on one side and a cobbled patchwork of countryside on the other. The late afternoon sun gilded church spires and the thatched roofs of cottages and cast deep shadows into the folds of the landscape. Abi saw none of it. Sprawled out on one of the benches, head part buried in a cushion, she pretended to be asleep. Her eyes were still hot and swollen from the tears she'd shed the previous night.

She had loved Edinburgh. Loved the tiered buildings which, despite their dark stone, managed to look cheerful even in the rain. Loved the galleries and museums, the shops, the cafes, the fact that you could walk from end to end of the city. The house? It was nice enough, a four-storey Georgian terrace in New Town. The one before (an Elizabethan manor with towering leaded windows and a coat of arms) had been more impressive. And the one before that, the mill with its constant accompaniment of rushing water had been exciting. It was just that each time they moved on she had to say goodbye to everything that had been part of her life for the past year or so. The few friends she'd made (who always promised to keep in touch but after a month or two gave up), the local shops and shopkeepers, the streets, the countryside, the walks that she'd grown familiar with. This time she had not even been allowed to enjoy the last weeks of the school term, with exams over and time for fun. Her mother had engineered a special dispensation because they were moving to England, but surely they could have waited. What was the hurry? Just her mother and Patrick being selfish as usual.

It hurt. And this time it hurt more than ever. Because of Tim MacKenzie, son of Graham and Muriel Mackenzie who right now would be moving into the Edinburgh house.

Tim. Tall, on the thin side, with that Scottish combination of light ginger hair and freckles that she had always disliked until now. They had hit it off right away. She had made him coffee while Patrick and her mother showed his parents around the house that first day three months ago. And from then on they had seen each other every day.

The new house was hundreds of miles away on the south coast, outside some village whose name meant nothing to her. Tim had said he would try to get a summer job near her, but what if he couldn't? Unless he hitchhiked he could never afford to come and see her. She clenched her eyes against another onrush of tears. Their relationship was so new, so fragile. How could it survive the distance between them? Just like everyone else she had known, he would probably give up and disappear from her life.

And there was nothing she could do about it. This was what her mother and Patrick did. They bought dilapidated

7

properties that no one wanted and turned them into something that everyone wanted. They'd been doing it for six years now. Living like nomads. They would probably still be doing it when they were old and decrepit.

If only they would stay in one place like normal people. But as soon as one house was looking good Patrick got that dreamy look in his eyes, the FOR SALE boards went up and he was looking for another wreck.

If only the wrecks could be closer together so that she could have something – or someone – permanent in her life.

If only.

Josh didn't care, but then, he was only ten and he found it all exciting. The constant moves, the new places, the new schools. He made friends easily and instantly, and it didn't bother him to leave them behind. There were always new people to meet. He had only dim memories of the time when Dad, their real Dad, was there and they had a warm, comfortable home, a garden where you could plant something and actually still be around to see it flower. And friends. Dad and friends. What was their life without either?

No, this life was her mother's and Patrick's choice, not hers. Well, she had plans now. She had her own bank account, her own passport, and as soon as she'd saved enough money she would be gone.

'Nearly there,' Patrick called back from the driver's seat. 'This is Bridport. Supposed to be pretty lively. Look, there's a street market and a brass band.'

She took a deep shuddering breath and sat up to glance through the window.

Great. As if a few crappy stalls and a group of fat men blowing trumpets would make up for everything. But in any case the musicians were packing away their instruments and stallholders were tossing unsold goods into their vans, although the pavements still bustled with locals and holidaymakers. She saw several groups of teenagers, arms round each other's shoulders, waiting to claim the streets for their own.

She turned away and glared at the back of Patrick's head, resenting his excitement. You could always tell when the adrenalin of a new project set in. His dark brush-cut hair would stand on end, almost quivering with electricity and he couldn't keep still. Even now, he was shifting in his seat, his fingers tapping on the steering wheel as he whistled an accompaniment to Queen's 'Another One Bites The Dust' on the radio.

**

Patrick was happy. He was starting a new adventure. A new dream. He had big plans for this one. It would be, he determined, the best yet. His whistle paused as he was reminded that it might also be his last. Carol had been the partner he had longed for, someone not only willing but eager to share his lifestyle, his dreams. But now . . . Well, it was the nesting instinct, wasn't it? And what man could fight it?

He sighed. Having a child, a son, the fruit of your loins. It was a big deal, wasn't it? Everyone said so. And he would love the kid when it came, he supposed, he would try to give it everything it desired, but did it really have to start its life in a permanent home with a nursery and all the paraphernalia that they advertised at Mothercare? Did it need to stay put in one place all its life? What if it had his genes? What if it was born with that itch that no amount of scratching could cure? He was only two generations removed from the Romany life. To wander the country - and to make money whilst doing it - that was his idea of perfection.

He remembered his old Gran, long dead now, and her tales of bringing up his own father and the other kids, four of them, in a caravan no bigger than an executive bathroom in a modern house. Youngest in a cardboard box, wrapped in an old blanket. The older ones top to tail in a cupboard bed.

He couldn't help feeling resentful of Carol's sudden and devastating determination to make the new house their permanent home. And the pregnancy itself. Her responsibility, wasn't it? She could have taken better care, it was not as if they couldn't have waited a while. At thirty four he still didn't feel ready to be a father, and Carol was still only just in her forties. She still had a few fertile years in her.

She'd made him promise. This house would be their last project. This baby was to have a permanent home. But what about him, Patrick? What did she expect *him* to do? The chance of finding houses - the right houses, big splendid properties that had fallen on hard times, properties so dilapidated that no one else would consider them - within reasonable driving distance of Marshbank was remote.

'That's a big sigh!' said Carol.

'Just the long drive. Shoulders aching.'

It wasn't the money. He could buy half a dozen smaller ordinary properties. He and his team could update and improve them, put them back on the market and make a comfortable profit. But where was the fun in that? Where was the creativity? The artistry?

Still. Who knew? Maybe something would come up later, something really special that would tempt even a new mother out of her nest. If not - well, he'd think about that another time.

Meanwhile - he checked his SatNav. Another seven miles and they'd be there. His heart lifted and he began to sing.

'It's a new day, da de da da - da, de da da . . . and I'm feelin' good!' He took a hand off the steering wheel and caressed Carol's stomach.

'Don't,' she whispered.

'They can't see.'

He glanced back at Carol's two children. Josh, bouncing up and down, grinned at him but Abi's face was dark and thunderous. Patrick sighed. Over the years he had tried to connect with her. He'd even offered to send her to boarding school, but that hadn't suited her either. Pity her father hadn't taken her with him after the split. Life would have been a hell of a lot easier. Still. As long as he had Carol. He turned to her, suddenly anxious.

'*You're* happy with me, aren't you?'

She smiled and squeezed his arm. 'Of course.'

He lowered his voice. 'You had such a different life with Michael.'

'Empty. Miserable.'

'I don't think Abi would agree with you. She'd swap me for her Dad like a shot.' He waited. 'Maybe she'd be better off with him.'

'No, never! Abi only remembers the good times.'

He sighed again.

High hedges brushed the windows of the Hymer as he turned on to a track barely wide enough to accommodate the huge vehicle. At the end of the track a pair of wrought iron gates hung at crazy angles off their posts, pointing the way along a stony moss covered drive. The house stood alone, long abandoned to the elements, its windows blinkered by curtains of ivy, its paintwork faded and blistered, its red brick facade disfigured by lichen, but to Patrick it offered a challenge that he accepted with delight.

Grabbing a bunch of old fashioned keys from the glove box, he was out of the van in a flash. He turned and beamed.

'This is it! Marshbank. Isn't she a beauty?'

Two

Ghosts can walk through walls. Through locked doors. I'd read that when I still had books to read. And one morning when the sun was bright, when fresh white clouds were scudding past the attic's tiny window and birds were chattering on the roof, I walked over to the locked door, closed my eyes and passed through it.

That first time shocked me. The house seemed as much a ghost as I myself. Cobwebs hung like gauze curtains across the narrow stairs down to the first floor. The walls were grimy and damp. There was a smell of decay. And death. The death of so many small animals, birds and insects over the years. All trapped within the empty house, like myself.

I passed silently through the rooms below, where the bright wallpapers had lost their colour and pattern and the wooden floors were blanketed with dust as thick and soft as cotton wool. Where were the curtains? The rugs?

The beds? The chairs and sofas? No one had lived here for years.

Only me.

In the kitchen I recognised the green and cream cooker, the quarry tiles, now cracked and blackened. Nothing had changed, everything had changed, since I was last free to eat a meal at that old wooden table.

After a brief struggle Patrick managed to open the front door and he and Carol disappeared inside, Josh jigging impatiently at their heels.

Abi hung back. It had been too much to expect the new wreck to be set amongst other houses, to have a front door from which Abi could step out and be surrounded by other people. Oh no, Marshbank was remote from everything. And big. Patrick liked the challenge of big houses. The bigger the better.

'Come on, Abi.' called her mother, her voice high with excitement.

Already the iPads were out and she and Patrick were taking photographs, making notes. They were a good team, Abi had to admit. Patrick had trained as an architect and Carol was an interior designer. They could glance at a ratty old room and immediately visualise it as something perfect and beautiful.

All Abi could see were sagging ceilings, peeling paint and fungi growing up the damp walls.

'I really like Edwardian architecture,' said Carol. 'Such large square rooms, so much light. It's going to look fantastic! What d'you think, Abi?

'I think it's a mess,' she said flatly. 'How long has it been empty?'

'Over seventy years,' said Patrick. 'Which meant we got it really cheap.'

'It smells.' She wrinkled her nose, wondering how long it had been since any other humans had stepped inside. She imagined a tomb would smell like this. One of those old family vaults with half a dozen coffins inside, some of them open to expose the dead bodies. But this wasn't a horror movie, this was Patrick's and Carol's latest project, and as usual they were like two kids let loose in Legoland.

She set off to explore on her own. Twenty two rooms on three floors, Patrick had told her. She wandered into the kitchen. Perhaps it had been the latest thing all those years ago, some woman's pride and joy, but now decades of rust and dust and grime blanketed every surface. Everything would have to go – the rusted iron stove, its oven door hanging open from one hinge, the cracked and water-stained sink, the blackened and uneven floor tiles, the tin cupboards, their green and cream paint just recognisable beneath the dirt. A job for the team when they arrived. She opened one of the cupboards. There was something inside, something that could once have been a loaf of bread, half gnawed by mice or rats before it fossilized.

She peeped into what must have been the drawing

room. Huge glass doors with windows either side looked out on to what would once have been a lawn. A carved wooden fireplace still wore most of its art nouveau lily-patterned tiles. Patrick would treasure those. The ornate ceiling had mouldered and crumbled, much of its plaster now masking the wooden parquet floor. There were footprints across the floor, she noticed. Not Patrick's or Carol's. Someone else had been here not too long ago. The property agent, she supposed. Or maybe a tramp.

The wide, once grand, central staircase creaked ominously as she climbed it. On the landing a small door opened on to another flight of stairs, narrow and twisty, rising up to the top floor. The attics. This would have been where the servants slept and where travel trunks, old furniture and things like cradles and cots no longer needed would have been stored.

The furthest attic looked out over the back garden, only it wasn't a garden any more, just a tangle of brambles and overgrown shrubs with dead brittle branches. There was something that might have been an orchard at the far end.

The room itself was in a poor state. Old wallpaper, faded to a dirty beige, hung in strips from the walls, two of the panes in the tiny window were boarded over, several of the floorboards were splintered, and there were generations of dead flies everywhere.

She turned to leave. But something drew her back. She stood in the centre of the room and turned slowly. It was so tiny, barely space for more than a table and a chair, and even cleaned up and the boards removed from the window, the light wouldn't be brilliant. And yet . . . She listened to the silence that was not quite silence. It seemed ridiculous – it *was* ridiculous, and yet the room seemed to be welcoming her. Inviting her to stay.

She nodded. 'Alright,' she said. 'Let's see how it goes.'

In each house she had chosen a private space to write her stories and, she had to admit, Patrick had always been willing to make that space habitable for her.

She had written her first book when she was ten, after her Dad had moved to New York and after Patrick had moved Mum, Josh and herself to the mill in Lancashire. It had forty pages, handwritten on both sides. Her heroine was the mill owner's daughter who helped to weigh the sacks of corn and to sweep up the chaff after milling. She was the same age as Abi and had the same long fair hair and blue eyes. Abi was obsessed with ballet at the time, and her mother had arranged for her to join a class in the nearest town. Of course the miller's daughter didn't do ballet, she was more of a clog dancer, but otherwise they were the same.

When Patrick bought the Tudor manor in Sussex she wrote about a young girl who sewed samplers and played the lute and wore a ruffle around her neck.

And in Edinburgh – but she had never finished that story. She had planned a fairytale ending and that was not going to happen.

She supposed in all her books she had really been writing about herself, and doubtless the next one would be no different. Well, who else could she write about?

17

She checked her phone. Still nothing from Tim. Should she call him? Her fingers hovered, but then she closed the phone. No. He must call first. Prove that he cared, that he still wanted them to be together.

'You can't possibly work here, it's horrible!' her mother protested when she saw the attic. 'Why don't you find a room on the first floor? Come and look.'

'I want this one.'

'Why?'

How could she explain, when she herself didn't really know why?

'Well, at least it's summer,' her mother sighed. 'You'd freeze here in the winter.'

Patrick looked equally baffled but he didn't try to change Abi's mind.

'I'll sort it in the morning,' he promised. 'Meanwhile . . . ' He had gone back to the Hymer and was now waving a bottle of champagne and four glasses. 'A toast. To Marshbank and all who sail in her!' He sloshed champagne into the glasses, full to the brim for himself and Carol, half full for Abi, and a careful inch for Josh.

Abi wrinkled her nose as the bubbles hit it. She didn't like champagne and she certainly didn't want to celebrate arriving at yet another project, but Patrick delighted in the ceremony. And her mother – she delighted in Patrick. Abi tipped her glass and let the champagne trickle to the floor, creating tiny ribbons in the dust. Her mother had got what she wanted. And Abi had lost everything.

Patrick's regular team, Harry the plumber, Jake the electrician, and Brandon and Marek for everything else, arrived a few hours later. Harry was driving the big van, with Brandon seated alongside him and a trailer hooked on behind. Jake followed with the battered old caravan the team slept in at night, and half an hour later Marek turned up in Patrick's car.

All the vehicles were now parked behind the house in the old yard where once there had been stables.

Briefly, Abi was relieved to see them. They were the only familiar people in her life now. Harry and Jake treated her like a favourite niece, and Brandon, who was about twenty years younger, treated her like a kid sister. Marek, whose English was still laboured, waved a hand in greeting.

The routine was the same each time. A few essentials for the house (a small fridge, a microwave, kitchen bits, crockery and cutlery, cardboard boxes packed with tinned food and ready meals, a couple of heaters) would be unpacked from the trailer. While there was no electricity a generator would be set up so that they could cook and keep warm.

Only when the house was fully habitable would their furniture be taken out of storage and delivered. It was usually six months or more before the family could begin to spread out and live like normal people.

And then it would all start again. The house would be put on the market while Patrick scouted for another project. The house would be sold, the furniture put back in store and they would be off again. Nothing changed. Nothing remained unchanged. This was her life, Abi thought bitterly.

After Josh, wild with excitement, had taken the team on a tour of the house, it was time for dinner. The men had brought in chairs and a folding table from the van, and Carol was heating up tins of tomato soup and buttering bread for cheese and pickle sandwiches. There was orange juice or lager to drink, and dessert would be a choice of bananas or apples.

Abi shredded a sandwich into tiny pieces and discarded a banana after a single bite. The taste was cloying and the texture was like wet papier mache. Looking up, she saw Patrick watching her.

'We'll go into Lyme Regis tomorrow, Abi. Have a slap up lunch to celebrate the new house, eh?'

'What's to celebrate?' she muttered, pushing aside her plate. She stood up. 'I'm off to bed,' she announced.

'Hey, it's only eight o'clock,' said Brandon. 'Stay and have some fun. There's a pub twenty minutes away. D'you fancy a walk?'

'With you? No thank you.' She wanted to hurt someone, and the words slipped out, but when she saw the shock on his face she wished she could swallow them back.

'I'm sorry – I'm just tired. We had an early start. Night, all.' And she was gone.

Back at the Hymer she slipped into a onesie and curled

up in her berth. She and Josh shared the tiny bedroom behind the kitchen and shower. She hoped he wouldn't disturb her when the others finished their celebration. Celebration! If she had enough money she would leave right now.

Too tense for sleep, she played through a scene she had imagined many times before. Herself boarding a plane. Her father waiting outside the barrier at John F Kennedy airport. His arms enfolding her as they met. His face was a little blurred – it was so long since she had seen him – but he was smiling, always smiling.

She glanced at her watch. What time was it in New York? Three in the afternoon. He would be at home. She had his number.

'Abi? This is a surprise. How are you? Look, I can't talk right now. We're just on our way to friends. Catch up tomorrow, eh? I'll phone you – let's see, ten a.m. here, three p.m. your time – is that OK? Good? Hugs from me and Donna. Bye, Honey!'

And he was gone.

Did people's accents change that much when they moved to another country? Dad sounded one hundred percent American. In fact, he sounded like a stranger. Which he almost was, of course. Nearly six years since he and her mother divorced, and in that time she had seen him twice. The first summer he had sent for her and the two of them had spent two wonderful weeks exploring Manhattan, the Rockefeller Center, Times Square and Central Park. But then he had sent her home and it was

21

another eighteen months before she saw him again. Since then there had been nothing but a handful of short, unsatisfactory phone calls, the occasional video call with poor reception, and her birthday and Christmas presents, which rarely matched either her age or her interests.

But it would all be different once they were together again.

The motorhome door opened and the floor vibrated slightly with Josh's footsteps. She listened to him scrubbing his teeth, gargling water (a new accomplishment), breathing heavily as he shed his shoes, pants and sweater.

'Josh?' she whispered, when he had leapt into the bunk opposite hers. 'Do you remember your Daddy? Do you remember him playing with us in the garden?'

He thought for some time. 'Yes, but I was only little then.'

'He used to give you rides on his back. Sometimes he'd be your horse. Other times he'd pretend to be an elephant, do you remember?'

'Did I like that?'

'Of course. Would you like him to come back, Josh?'

He turned to her, startled. '*Is* he coming back?'

'No,' she said quickly.

'That's OK then. We've got Patrick now.'

'Do you like Patrick?'

22

'Yes, but I like Harry best. I wish Harry was my Dad.'

Small children forget, Abi told herself after Josh had gone to sleep, but she couldn't forget. She still loved her father. She hoped he still loved her. She missed him.

Three

Dead people don't sleep. How can they?

You need a biological clock to tell you when you're tired and when you're full of energy. You need a body to tell you when you're hungry or thirsty. I don't have that. On the other hand I don't experience any of the bad things about having a body. I don't feel cold, I don't feel pain, I don't get headaches or tummy ache. I don't cry.

But for a long long time I wanted desperately to be able to sleep. To escape from all the bad memories, the loneliness, the fear of drifting through eternity all alone.

Eventually I found a way to switch off from everything. It's not sleep, but it's as close as I can manage. This is what I do. I curl up in the darkest corner of the attic – there's no bed, no furniture at all, he cleared it out the very next day - so I curl up on the floor facing the wall and I will my mind to empty of all thoughts. It's a sort of self-hypnosis, I suppose.

At first it was difficult, but I persevered, and now I can remove myself at will for quite long periods. Of course, I don't have a watch or clock to check that precisely but I believe that sometimes I'm 'asleep' for days, perhaps even weeks.

Which is why I didn't see the girl until she was already established in my attic. I just came back to consciousness one evening (the sun was low in the sky, sending shafts of golden light across the room) and there she was! Sitting on a chair, a table in front of her, on the table a shiny box thing. Some sort of typewriter, I thought, because her fingers were racing over it.

Hello? I called. Hello?

Is she a ghost? No. If she was a ghost she would hear me. She would turn and we would greet each other, with laughter and thankfulness.

No, she is alive. Oh, if only I was alive too.

As promised, Patrick had ripped away the boards that were nailed across the attic's tiny window, rigged an extension lead up through the ceiling below for Abi's laptop and a lamp, and lugged a spare foldaway table and chair up the stairs.

Carol had helped to tear the loose wallpaper from the walls and had hung an old curtain at the window. Later she brought up some brightly patterned cushions and a rolled up poster of a Matisse painting. They came from the small store of items that she used to bring a

25

temporary touch of home to the houses they renovated.

'I was going to put these in the sitting room, but I decided your need was greater than mine!'

'Thanks,' Abi muttered.

'Anything to please,' Carol said lightly. 'You know I want you to be happy.'

Then why did you drag me away? Again?

When he saw the attic Josh, of course, wanted to stake his claim.

'This could be my den,' he announced. 'Look, it's just the right size for me. You can write anywhere, Abi.'

'Go and find your own den,' she snapped.

Already, the little room was welcoming her.

She set up her laptop on the rickety table and started a new folder.

Marshbank (working title).

Her heroine would be sixteen years old. Slim, with blue eyes and long fair hair. A servant in a large Edwardian house. The year? Say, 1917. Her name would be . . . Tabitha? Louisa? Henrietta? Isabella? Yes, Isabella. A bit fancy, perhaps, for a servant girl of the time, Ethel would be more suitable. No, stick with Isabella. The girl's mother had been a reader and had seen the name in a romantic novel.

The attic. This would be Isabella's bedroom where she

26

retired late at night, exhausted after cleaning fireplaces, hauling buckets of coal, dusting and polishing, fetching and carrying - oh yes, Abi had watched Downton Abbey. She stared around the tiny room, replacing the old faded wallpaper with white distemper, placing a narrow iron-framed bed with a thin horsehair mattress opposite the door, perhaps a bible on a stool beside it. Under the window a cheap pine washstand complete with enamel bowl and jug.

The first two pages of text flew from her fingers. And then she sat back to read what she had written, but before she could start she heard a loud scream from somewhere below. Her mother? Abandoning her laptop she flew down the stairs.

'What is it? What's wrong?' she asked Patrick, who was also hurrying down the stairs.

Carol was in the kitchen, her face white, her hands trembling.

'It's in there.' She pointed with a toe at one of the old kitchen cupboards. 'It's alive.'

'A rat?' Abi asked.

Carol shook her head. 'No, a spider. One of those huge hairy ones with big muscular black legs.' She shuddered.

'Oh, for Heaven's sake, Mum. What are you doing, renovating old houses, if you're scared of creepy crawlies? There are probably whole colonies here, crawling around all the bedrooms, climbing up your legs, abseiling down on to your head - '

'Don't! Stop it!' Carol put her hands over her ears and ran from the room.

'That was cruel, Abi. Especially now. Don't you know - ?

'What?'

'Nothing,' said Patrick. 'OK, I'm going to get some insect spray and that'll get rid of them. Meanwhile, you can make your Mum a strong cup of tea.'

The urge to write had faded. Irritated by the interruption and her mother's silliness Abi was at a loose end. Everyone else seemed to have a task, most of them involving a lot of noise. Even Josh was employed, handing tools to Harry while the plumber worked on reconnecting the water supply.

Recently Carol and Patrick had tried to involve her. She had resisted furiously. She would sooner sabotage the whole project. But sometimes, like now, she wished she had something to do, other than her writing. She was lonely, isolated by her own stubbornness, she acknowledged to herself, but how else could she show her disapproval?

Outside, she wandered through the garden and down to the orchard. There seemed to be an extra quietness here. It was the lack of bird calls, she realised. The old trees, planted when the house was built, she surmised, had intertwined their gnarled limbs, forming a canopy that kept out all but the smallest patterns of sunlight. She shivered.

She closed her eyes, willing herself into the past, recalling her favourite memory. The garden at Oaklands, the only home she had known with her mother and father. A summer day that seemed to last forever. The fresh hay-like smell of newly mown grass. Bees, humming contentedly, plunging deep into the tunnels of the foxgloves that her mother grew specially for them. The blackbirds that nested every year in the beech hedge. Her mother, bringing out a tray of home-made scones and home-made lemonade. Her father playing horse, with Josh, then four years old, the rider on his back.

Everyone smiling. Everyone loving everyone else .

If only she could turn the clock back six years.

'Bit of a mess, isn't it?'

It was Harry. He had followed her down the garden with two mugs of coffee.

'All these old fruit trees. Almost barren now, need grubbing out.'

It was an unwanted interruption but she couldn't be cross with Harry. He was the nearest to a father that she had now, and she knew he cared about her.

'We had a lovely garden where we used to live – I mean, me, Josh and Mum and my Dad. They even put it on Gardeners' World once. I wish - '

'No good wishing for the past, lass. Those days are gone. You have to look forward. And you don't want to upset your Mum, do you? She loves you - '

'No, she doesn't. All she cares about is Patrick and these horrible houses. She doesn't care that she's ruining my life!'

Ali turned away so that Harry wouldn't see the tears that were threatening to fall.

'Talk to her. Tell her how you feel. She cares, of course she does.'

Did she? Was it possible that her mother just hadn't realised how empty Abi's life had become?

'Why don't you go and have a chat now?' Harry urged her. 'Can't do any harm, can it?'

She smiled at him, comforted. Perhaps he was right. What harm could it do?

'Were you ever married, Harry?' she asked, suddenly curious.

His face closed. 'Aye. A long time ago.'

'What happened?' She waited. He sighed.

'I used to drink. My wife, Angie, she chucked me out.'

'Oh. I'm sorry.   But you don't drink now.' She recollected that she had never seen him with the cans of lager the other men consumed like water, and on their trips to the pub he usually had a glass of orange juice in his hand.

'Couldn't you get together again?'

'She died.'

'I'm sorry. Did you have any children?'

'Two boys,' he said. Reluctantly. 'All in the past now. They both live abroad. One in Texas, the other in Japan. They don't even remember me. Or want to.'

'Their loss. I think you'd be a wonderful father.'

'Thanks, but too many years have passed.'

He closed his eyes, as if in pain. Abi stared at him, thinking what a mess life could be. She wondered which was worse – her loss of her father, or Harry's loss of his wife and children?

He opened his eyes and touched her cheek gently with a calloused hand, wiping away the tears that still clung there.

'So, don't do what I did. Don't leave it too late.'

Four

Abi. Her name is Abi. I move to where I can watch her. Watch her face, see how she chews her lower lip when she pauses to think of more words, listen to her humming as she types, wait for her smile when she's pleased with something she's written.

How wonderful to be an author. I used to make up stories in my head but with no way to record them they were easily forgotten.

Soon – too soon – she is gone again. But she has left her typing box open. I drift across and read the words she has written.

Marshbank. Yes. But – Isabella? No, that's not right. Isabella! In my attic. Sleeping in my attic! No, Abi should write about me. Me! For hundreds – thousands – of days and nights I've been alone and forgotten. What happened to me is far more important than a tale about a servant girl called Isabella.

I must find a way to make her see that.

Abi had not yet decided to speak to her mother. Whatever Harry said, would it really make a difference? She hovered in the hall. One of the team had turned on his I-Pad and music blared out. An old T-Rex hit.

'I've been looking everywhere for you,' said Carol, appearing from the room she had turned into a temporary office.

'What now?' wondered Abi.

The room, smaller than the drawing room, had a huge bay window and an original fireplace with shelves and a mirror above it. Later it would have a leather-topped partners' desk, floor to ceiling bookshelves either side of the French window and cream-painted panelling on the other walls. Lamps, rugs, paintings. All the accessories that helped to sell a house.

Patrick had already stripped off some of the old paint to see what was underneath. Abi inhaled the heady smell of turpentine in the air. At the moment the only furniture was the battered oak table from the kitchen, plus three folding chairs.

A bottle of elderflower juice and two glasses stood on the table. Her mother filled them. She was nervous and the bottle chattered against the glasses. She stared down at them for a long time.

'Mum?'

33

'Patrick wanted to be here as well, but I thought it would be better if I told you myself.'

'Told me what?' asked Abi. She had a sudden thought. 'You're not ill, are you?'

'No, no. The thing is . . .'

Was she blushing? Yes, her mother was blushing!

'I'm expecting a baby.'

What?

'I know. It was a shock for me too.'

More than a shock. An embarrassment!

'You can't be. You're too old!'

'I'm only forty two. Lots of women have babies in their forties. It - we hadn't planned - I know it's a lot to take in, but it'll be nice, won't it? A sweet little baby boy - '

'A boy? How long have you known, then?'

'About eight weeks.'

'Eight weeks? And you didn't tell me until now?'

'We wanted to break it to you gradually, I know how you teenagers react sometimes when their ancient parents produce another child. We didn't want you to feel embarrassed with your friends.'

'Friends? What friends? All these years - I've never had time to make friends before we're all off again.'

'Well . . . it'll be different now. We're going to stay put.

There'll be time for you to prepare for your exams, get into a university - '

Abi felt the bitterness rise into her throat, sour and stinging.

'So this baby - this sweet little baby boy - he's going to have a proper home, he's going to go to the same school for as many years as it takes, he'll be able to make friends and *keep* them.' She glared at her mother. 'You never stayed put for me after you and Dad split up. You never considered that I might like to settle in one place, put down roots, go to school, have a life!'

'Abi, it's our business, it's how we make a living. We thought you and Josh would enjoy it. I thought it might help if you were missing your father.'

'Josh was so young, he hardly remembers him. But me - you took everything away from me. My Dad, the home I was born in, the garden, my school, my friends - and what for? To camp in one mouldy old house after another, with no friends, no neighbours even.'

Abi was almost spitting with rage.

'Did you know I had a boyfriend in Edinburgh?'

'What? For Heaven's sake, Abi, why didn't you tell me?'

'What was the point? You and Patrick would still have wanted to move on. But now - Well, Patrick is going to have a son of his own and he's willing to stay put for that.'

'Abi, stop it! The chief reason we're going to stay in this house is because of my age. I've got to take a bit more care, and I won't have the stamina I've had in the past. Anyway, I thought, we both thought, you enjoyed all this, all the excitement of new places. Why didn't you say something before if you weren't happy?'

'When? When we've just arrived at a new place, or when Patrick's got that gleam in his eye again and we're off without warning to some other godforsaken dump? It wouldn't be so bad if they were closer together and I didn't have to start again each time.'

'Oh Abi! I didn't realise you hated our lifestyle so much, I just put your moods down to teenage hormones. We'll make it up to you, I promise. And I promise we'll stay here - if not forever, at least until you and Josh are both settled.'

'Are you and Patrick going to get married?'

'No, we - '

'I suppose it doesn't matter anyway, does it? You and Dad were married and that didn't last, did it?'

'That wasn't my fault. It was - '

Carol stood up, arms stretched for an embrace. Abi backed away.

'I hate you! And Patrick. And don't think I'm ever going to babysit. I hate your baby too!'

***

She found Patrick happily contemplating the gutted kitchen. The cream and green metal cupboards had been stacked carefully outside the back door.

'Art Deco - worth a bit now. There's a reclamation company near here. I've just done a deal with them.'

'Mum's told me about the baby. *Your* baby!'

Patrick's smile disappeared.

'You're pleased, aren't you? It won't make any difference with you and Josh – your Mum will still love you both as much.'

Love! Love meant caring. Love meant putting your children before yourself, making them happy.

'So why haven't you asked Mum to marry you?'

He shrugged. 'You know why. I'm a Catholic. In God's eyes your Mum and your Dad are still husband and wife.'

'My Dad's married again, and he and Donna haven't been struck by lightning.'

'Who knows what the future may bring? Punishment doesn't always come immediately.'

'Oh, grow up, Patrick. You're not a little boy learning your catechism at your mother's knee. People marry, divorce, re-marry in their millions and often they're happier second time around. My Dad and Donna are happy.'

'How d'you know? You think he'd tell you?'

'Yes! We talk every day.'

But they didn't. He still hadn't returned her last call. And looking back she couldn't remember a time when he had called her first. But he was a busy man, she told herself, with many demands on his time. An important man. Far more important than Patrick, who was more like a kid playing at life than a proper grown-up like her Dad.

If she lived with Dad and Donna she would be happy, she knew it. She would go to school, and then to college, she would have lots of friends, the whole of New York would be her playground. She still hadn't saved enough for the flight, but perhaps Dad would help her. She checked the time. Two thirty. Nine thirty in New York. She could phone him now, before he got busy. She would tell him about Mum's baby, tell him how unhappy she was, ask him to pay for a plane ticket.

'Sorry,' her father said when he answered. 'I was supposed to call you, wasn't I? Meetings, meetings! As soon as one finishes I'm called to another.'

So what was wrong with calling her in the evening, from his home? she wondered briefly.

'Anyway, here I am, talking to my favourite daughter.'

Your *only* daughter.

'I do think about you, you know. Miss you. Remember that time when - '

She cut across him.

'Mum's having a baby!'

There was silence at the other end. Quite a long silence.

At last: 'Well, ain't that a coincidence!'

Abi suddenly felt cold.

'What? What d'you mean?' But already she knew.

'Donna and me, we're expecting our first. In the Fall.'
He laughed.

A wave of dizziness hit her.

'I have to go,' she said, and ended the call.

Five

I waited and waited but Abi didn't come. I wanted to search for her but I was frightened.

Once, a long time ago, I ventured out of the attic, out of the house. I drifted along the cliffs above the sea and encountered a family. Father, mother, two children and a dog. They all, except the dog, walked right through me. It was not pleasant. For each one a jolt, a flare of heat that disappeared as quickly as it came, leaving me shaken and scared.

The dog. I'm sure it saw me. It barked and barked, frightening me even more before it backed away, almost falling over the cliff.

'Come here, you little tyke,' shouted the father. He grabbed the dog's collar and attached its lead. And then they were gone.

I think a couple of seagulls saw me too. They came

winging in to land, scorched almost to a halt in mid-air and went streaking out to sea again, screeching and screaming.

I turned away, wanting nothing more than to hurry back to my attic. It might be my prison but it was also my place of safety. What if I couldn't find my way back? What if I had to roam the huge outside world alone, unseen, unknown? No! The attic was my home. Home? Yes, what else could I call it?

I felt very lonely. My only hope of companionship was the possibility that I would one day meet another ghost.

But now there is Abi and I feel we could be friends. I just have to find a way to make her aware of me.

Abi had to get out. Feeling cold, sick, betrayed, she hunted for her bicycle and eventually found it in a tumbledown shed at the rear of the house. It was an effort to manhandle it past all Patrick's bits of machinery and out on to the drive.

'Want a hand?'

It was Harry, wandering round the overgrown garden with a mug of tea.

He glanced at his watch. 'So where are you off to?'

She looked away. 'Oh, nowhere particular, just a little ride. It's too noisy in there to concentrate.'

She had no idea where she was going, but anywhere would do. Anywhere away from her mother and Patrick.

She was hungry, she would miss lunch but she had money. She would cycle somewhere, maybe back to the town where she'd seen all those teenagers and buy her own slap-up lunch. What was it called? Bridport, that was it.

Harry laid a hand on her shoulder. 'Things will get better.'

No, they won't, she thought. They could only get worse.

In the High Street and down one of the side streets stalls had been set up. Of course, it was Saturday. Another market day. She turned off the High Street and cycled slowly down East Street, found a path at the end which bordered the narrow river. Wheeling her bike, she breathed in the warm midday air. She passed two horses in a field, who raised their heads and seemed pleased to see her. Beyond the bustle of the market all was still and quiet.

Following her nose she found herself back in the High Street. Some of the stallholders had gathered together and were drinking coffee. Her mouth dried and her stomach rumbled in sympathy.

'Where's the best place for a coffee?' she called.

A brawny young man in a singlet and patched jeans waved his paper cup. 'Here! Buy a burger and I'll treat you to one!'

'You're on. Thanks.'

While she drank the coffee and wolfed her burger she read the notices on the wall alongside the Town Hall. The wall was barely visible behind dozens of posters. Concerts, plays, films, art exhibitions, classes in everything from dance to mindfulness, all sorts of groups bidding for members.

It wasn't a bad town, she accepted, although grudgingly. Not a patch on Edinburgh, of course, but it seemed interesting - and friendly. So far.

No credit to Patrick or Mum, of course. All they were interested in was their latest house project and the new baby.

***

'Mum, I'm starving,' said Josh. 'Do we have to have sandwiches? Can't we have sausages? And bacon?'

The thought of cooking meat, any form of meat, turned Carol's stomach, but the men had eaten a sandwich lunch for three days without complaint.

'All right. Go round everyone up. Give me twenty minutes.'

When the hot food was ready and Patrick and the team assembled, she looked for Abi.

'Anyone seen her?'

'She took her bike from the shed,' said Harry. 'Expect she's gone exploring. Didn't she leave a note?'

Patrick came over to Carol.

'You worried?' he whispered.

'After the way she behaved yesterday - Yes, I am, rather.'

'I expect she's just out to let off a bit of steam,' he said. 'She'll be back by dinner time, you'll see.' But dinner time came and went and Abi was still absent.

Josh was upset. 'Has she run away?'

'Of course she hasn't run away,' Carol snapped. But had she? 'She's just gone to explore.'

'Can *we* go and explore?' he asked eagerly.

'I think we must stay here and wait. Don't worry,' she said, seeing his downcast face. 'Perhaps we'll all go out for a nice meal and a look round Lyme Regis or West Bay tomorrow. And I'm sure Abi will be back soon. Maybe you can stay up a little later tonight,' she added, which cheered him.

***

After dinner Carol and Patrick toured the house, preparing the next day's schedule of work for the team. Abi had still not returned by the time they reached the last of the attics.

'I don't like this room,' said Carol.

'Yes, not what I'd choose. Too dark, and way too small.'

'It's not just that. It's got – I don't know – some sort of atmosphere.'

'You're not going all fey on me, are you? Now that you're pregnant?'

44

Carol shivered. 'There's a draft coming from somewhere.'

'Lots of chinks around that window. I'll get Brandon to plug them up when he's got time.'

'I wish I could persuade her to use one of the rooms downstairs,' said Carol as they were leaving, 'but nothing I say gets through to her now.'

'Probably doesn't even like this attic,' said Patrick. 'Just likes being awkward. Don't worry about it. She'll settle down. Eventually,' he added, but his tone was doubtful.

***

Abi had enjoyed her afternoon. She had browsed amongst the High Street and East Street stalls, buying a couple of secondhand dvds, a hand printed silk scarf, a pendant set with a stone that might or might not be jade. She had bought a bag of plums and now she sat on a wall listening to the band, which she had to admit was very good, even if the music was old fashioned.

Around her people were chatting, laughing, arguing, sharing their food and drink. One couple, a boy and a girl no older than herself had formed their own small oasis amongst the crowd. Arms wrapped around each other, they were oblivious of everyone else.

Abi, no longer hungry, put aside her bag of plums. If only Tim were here. They had spoken at last, but only after she had phoned him. It was an unsatisfactory call, full of vague apologies. He'd tried a few pubs in Lyme

Regis and Bridport, but no luck, he said. All the summer vacancies were filled. Maybe Patrick could find something for him to do at Marshbank, Abi had suggested, even if it was just clearing the garden, but Tim's response was half-hearted, and pride wouldn't let her push him any further. It was over.

A middle-aged couple, grasping large baguettes and takeaway coffees, squeezed up beside her on the wall.

'We come every Saturday,' said the woman. She pointed with her baguette. 'That's our daughter, Jackie. The blonde one with the trumpet. She's been with the band for a year now.'

Abi stared at the girl, whose cheeks were inflating and deflating with the beat of the music. Were they supposed to do that? she wondered. They'd probably collapse like worn paper bags when she was thirty. But she couldn't suppress a surge of envy. It must be nice to belong to something. To be pals with so many others, sharing the same focus.

The band members played their last number and began to put their instruments away. Jackie's parents rushed to help her. The stalls were also packing up, stacking their goods into the vans parked alongside the pavements. With a sudden drop in spirits Abi stood with her bike in the emptying square outside the Town Hall and wondered what to do next.

'You on your own?'

A group of teenagers, also with bikes, had gathered across the square. One of them, a red haired girl with UP

THE GINGERS printed on her T shirt, wheeled her bike across.

'You on your own?' she repeated.

Abi nodded.

'On holiday?'

Abi shook her head. 'No. We've just moved here. I don't know anyone yet.'

'Well, come along with us if you like. We're cycling to West Bay.'

Abi had no idea where West Bay was, but wherever it might be, she wanted to go there. Who knew? These four girls and three boys could become her first friends - and with luck she'd be able to hang on to them.

West Bay was full of holidaymakers, seagulls, fishing boats and scuba divers. Abi loved it. The tang of salt, the aromas of grease and vinegar and fried onions, the stench of diesel from outboard motors, combined in her nostrils. She breathed in deeply.

'Where will you be going to school?' asked one of the other girls, a tiny slim brunette wearing the briefest of scarlet shorts and scarlet-rimmed sunglasses to match. She was the one the three boys hung around.

'Bridport, I think.'

The girl nodded. 'We're all there. I'm Lacey.' She waved a hand at the others. 'Craig, Mick, Anna, Lily, Jonathan and Tina.'

'So where were you before?' asked Tina, the red haired girl. Abi told them.

'Edinburgh! That's miles away!'

Abi sighed. 'Don't I know it!'

She told them about moving four times in six years, of having to live like gypsies.

'I wouldn't mind that,' said Tina. 'It's boring here.'

'I had to leave my boyfriend behind.'

'I'm free!' Mick, a tall, gangly boy with a floppy fringe, leered at her,

'Take no notice of him. He's the class clown!'

'Got any money?' asked Lacey. 'We're going to get fish and chips.'

'I'll pay. I've got plenty,' said Abi. Instantly she regretted the offer. Would they think she was trying to bribe them? Well, they'd be right, of course.

The others looked at each other.

'OK,' said Lacey carelessly

An hour passed. Two hours. They visited one of the local pubs, and again Abi paid. It was lemonade all round, but Jonathan produced a bottle of vodka from his rucksack and sloshed some into each glass.

The sun had disappeared. Abi shivered in the coolness of the evening. She stood up and had to cling to the edge of the table, her head swimming..

'I'd better go.'

'Can you find your way back?' asked Craig, a dark unsmiling boy who'd contributed nothing to the conversation so far.

Abi had no idea, but she nodded.

'Right at the end of the road, left and then right again. Straight all the way to Bridport,' said Jonathan.

No one offered to ride back with her, but Jonathan was right. The route was straightforward.

Not so straightforward was the route from Bridport back to Marshbank. She crossed a large roundabout and found herself in the main street. The market stalls and most of the visitors had gone but lights from the town's cafes and pubs spilled across the pavements.

She cursed herself for not checking the full address. Marshbank was not in a village but it would surely have a postcode. She could phone Patrick or her mother and then check it out in one of the pubs but she was reluctant to do so. No, she would find her way back on her own.

Six

Abi is still away. I steel myself to leave the attic and search downstairs. The mother and the man Abi calls Patrick are sitting at a table. The mother is upset. The Patrick man looks angry. Other men are there. I stay away from them. I don't trust men. Any men. How do I know they are not like him?

The boy is there. He seems frightened. He looks straight at me. But can he see me? I'm not sure.

They are talking about Abi. The mother looks worried. Or is she just pretending to worry? Mothers are good at that. Pretending. My mother pretended to love me, but she went away. Abandoned me.

Carol glanced at her watch. 'It's gone nine o'clock. Where is she?'

'God knows!' said Patrick.

'I expect she went to Bridport,' said Harry. 'She would have remembered the way.'

'But not necessarily the way back,' said Patrick, 'and it's getting dark.'

Josh was trying to control his tears. He didn't mind crying in front of his mother and Patrick, but not the other men. Not Harry. But he was scared. He tugged Patrick's arm.

'Do - do you think she's been kidnapped?'

'No, Josh. I think she's just in a temper and wants to upset us.'

'Don't say things like that to him,' Carol snapped.

'Well, it's true, isn't it?'

'I think she *has* run away,' Josh whispered.

'No, lad. Where would she run to?' said Harry.

'To New York. She's been saving up.'

Patrick and Carol looked at each other.

'Is that what she's told you?' asked Carol.

'No. I heard her talking to Tim. She said if you made her move again she'd get on a plane to Daddy.'

'Tim? Who's Tim?' Patrick looked from one to the other.

'Her boyfriend,' said Carol. 'She's only just told me. Mr and Mrs Mackenzie's son.'

'Well. There seems to be a lot we don't know about Abi,' said Patrick.

Josh was really crying now.

'She's probably on a plane already, and we'll never see her again!'

'No, Josh,' said Patrick. 'The nearest airport is miles away.' He stared out of the window at the darkening sky. It was beginning to rain. He turned to Carol. 'For Heaven's sake, phone her.'

But Abi's phone was turned off.

***

It was another half an hour before Abi gave up. Her legs were trembling with fatigue. Several times cars with headlights blazing had rushed past, almost driving her into the roadside hedge. It was like one of those nightmares where you struggled to reach your destination and never got there.

This was all *their* fault. Patrick and her Mum. If they had given her even a moment's consideration before they uprooted her, she wouldn't be out here, lost in the gathering dark, soaking wet and shivering despite the lingering warmth of the summer day.

She turned on her phone and called Patrick's number.

'Where are you?'

'I'm in a lane.'

'Which lane?'

She looked around her. 'I don't know. They all look the same, just hedges and fields.'

'Have you passed any houses?'

'There were a couple of cottages at the top of the hill.'

'Go back, speak to the owners, ask exactly where you are. Get a postcode.'

'You *will* come and get me, won't you? It's dark, and I'm - a bit wet.'

She heard Patrick sigh. 'Of course I'll come and get you. Phone me when you've been to the cottages.'

Cycling back up a steep hill was beyond her. It was another twenty minutes before she staggered up the path of the first cottage. The old couple who lived there were kind. They insisted on bringing Abi inside and feeding her with hot tea and a fairy cake while she phoned to give Patrick directions.

'Don't ever do that again,' Patrick said as he strapped Abi's bike to the roof rack. 'Your mother's almost hysterical and she needs -- ' He broke off. 'Go off on your own if you must, but always tell us where you'll be. It was an idiotic thing to do. You don't even know the area!'

'Sorry,' she muttered.

The rest of the drive took place in silence. She stole a glance at his tight lipped profile. He doesn't really care, she thought. I'm just the fly in his ointment, a pest that he has to put up with, part of the package that came with her mother.

53

Josh had been allowed to stay up. His face was tear-stained, Abi noticed. As soon as she came through the front door he rushed forward and hugged her.

'I thought you'd run away!'

'No,' she said. *But I will, soon. Very soon.*

The team were there. Harry shook his head in disgust. Brandon wouldn't even look at her.

I'm sorry, Abi said silently. She hadn't even thought about the men when she left that morning. They were her friends. Her only friends. The last people she'd want to upset.

'Let's leave explanations until tomorrow.' Carol's voice was a weary whisper. 'We're all tired. Let's all get to bed.'

***

The next morning Abi crept out of the van before the others were awake. She had no intention of answering questions over breakfast. She was sorry the men had been inconvenienced – they had most likely had to forego their nightly visit to the pub – and she wished she hadn't upset Josh, but she didn't care about her mother and Patrick.

In the house she grabbed a can of orange juice and a clutch of biscuits and climbed the stairs to the top floor.

It was warm in the attic. Airless. The sun slanted into the tiny room, highlighting a shaft of dust motes. Abi went over to the window but there was no way to open it. Once, perhaps, but at some time the casement had been screwed down. The screws were deep and rusted. She waited until she heard movement down below and then she phoned Patrick.

'Could one of the team come up and get this window open? Is Brandon busy?'

'So you're up there, are you? You know you've upset your Mum again?'

'She upset *me.*'

'Well, one of you had better put up the white flag. I'm sick of this.'

Abi was silent.

'Well, you'll have to wait. They're all busy right now. I'll send Brandon up later.'

After that the noise level from below seemed to increase, as if Patrick was displaying his displeasure, but within the hour Brandon appeared in the doorway.

Before she met Tim she'd had a bit of a crush on Brandon. But he was seven years older than her and all he thought about was beer and body building. She wondered what Patrick and her Mum would think if she made a play for him. At the very least, they'd be embarrassed.

The wood was old and rotten, and the screws were huge. She watched as he struggled to remove them.

'The size of them!' he said. 'Talk about overkill! And what was the point? No-one could climb up here and break in, and no-one's going to break out, are they?'

The muscles under his sleeveless tee shirt bulged and

rippled. He had long blonde hair, worn in a pony tail, an all-year-round tan and tattoos on both forearms. He looked as if he should be in a boy band.

Abi crept up behind him and laid a caressing hand on the back of his neck.

'Shit!' He dropped his screwdriver. 'Thought it was a ghost!'

'Do you believe in ghosts, Brandon?'

'You never know. It's a spooky old house, isn't it? So - did you want something?'

He glanced at her, a little embarrassed. She gazed back. She couldn't do it. A spot of vengeance on Mum and Patrick wasn't worth the risk of losing one of her only friends.

'I just wanted to say that I'm sorry about the other night. I was feeling angry about something and I took it out on you.'

He smiled. 'It's OK. I know you love me really. We're mates. Right?'

'Right!' said Abi, relieved.

At last the remaining screws were out and with much creaking and groaning the window was pushed open.

'I'll have to do a proper job on that when I've time. It's likely to fall off and land on someone's head below, the state of it.'

He glanced around the room at the dingy faded

56

wallpaper, the dark brown stain on the ceiling where the roof had leaked, the cracks beneath the window, the splintered floorboards.

'Don't understand why you want to hide yourself up here, Abi. It's a ruin. God knows when Patrick will get round to sorting it. And so tiny. It's like being in a prison cell.'

A prison cell? Maybe. And maybe that's what she wanted. Somewhere to lock herself away from those who were making her life miserable.

When Brandon had gone, she clicked on her laptop and opened the file for her new book.

She read the first half dozen pages with dissatisfaction. Everything she had written so far, she decided, was drivel. Of course, she had every excuse for writing drivel. Her life was falling apart. Wasn't it bad enough that her mother was expecting a baby? Neither she nor Patrick would have any time for Ali's problems once it was born. But her Dad! Her escape route! She would be the last person he and Donna wanted in their life now. Their first child together. They were all too old, anyway. Well, not Donna, she was only twenty five.

Tears blurred her eyes. She blinked and stared at the screen again. Her prose was flat and boring, and the heroine's name which she had liked so much yesterday now seemed even more inappropriate. Another name popped into her head. Helen.

And did she really want to write about Edwardian times? She would just be echoing the story she had

57

started but not finished in Edinburgh. Patrick had said Marshbank had been empty for over seventy years. So, how about the 1940s? Her heroine could have been growing up during the war years. Planes overhead, bombs, rationing. It could be quite exciting.

Decision made, she erased everything she had keyed in the day before.

Seven

The man has gone and I have Abi to myself.

Seeing her in my attic again - a girl, a girl like me - fills me with joy. She doesn't make any sign that she is aware of me. She doesn't scream. Or even look uncomfortable. But why is she crying? As I watch she dashes the tears away and clicks her typing box. She presses something else and music suddenly blares.

She looks nice. Different. Perhaps it's her clothes. A black top with scarlet words printed across it. 'TRUST ME, I'M A WRITER'. And trousers, the sort a boy might wear. Or a workman. Although I don't think either would wear trousers so tight. How could anyone bend down or sit in them?

I move behind her and stare over her shoulder. She presses another key and her book is there, waiting. But everything she had typed before has disappeared. All I see is the title and a date.

Marshbank (Working Title) by Abigail Stratton.

2nd draft June 2019.

*I stare at the words, stunned, disbelieving. No! It can't be. Seventy six years since I died. I am ninety two years old! If I could see myself - If Abi could see me - would she see an old lady? No! I am still me, I am still sixteen, a young girl. And Abi is a young girl too. We can still be friends. We **will** be friends.*

But now she is typing again and suddenly – I see my name! Helen! I want to laugh! I want to cry! I want to jump up and down! I can't do any of those things. I stretch out my hand and gently touch her shoulder. I can't feel anything, except that fleeting sensation of warmth. As for Abi, there's no sign that she's aware of me, but in her mind, in her soul, a part of me must be present.

And the book. From now on it's going to be about me. Me!

If I'd been able to cry I would have cried then, wild with an emotion that I could hardly recognise, it was so long since I had last experienced it.

Carol put down her fork and pushed her plate away. A week had gone by and they were still eating makeshift meals. Tinned cream of mushroom soup, microwaved lasagnes, bananas. Orange juice for Abi, Mum, Josh and Harry. Lager or beer for Patrick and the rest of the team. The men were in good form, relaxing after a strenuous day, telling jokes, arguing about football. Brandon and

Jake were ribbing Marek because he supported Arsenal, whose centre forward reminded him of his younger brother back home in Bulgaria.

She glanced at Abi.

'I've a free day tomorrow and the weather forecast is good. I thought we could take the car into Dorchester, you, me and Josh. I hear there are some good shops - '

'Wow! Yes, please!' shouted Josh. 'There's a dinosaur museum - Harry told me.'

'You two go,' said Abi.

Carol sighed. 'Please come. We're still a family, nothing will spoil that.'

'Actually, I want to get on with my book. I've made some changes.'

''So what's it about?'

Abi shrugged. 'Nothing much so far.'

Carol sighed. How long was it since she and Abi had enjoyed a normal conversation?

'When's it set?' asked Harry, who had always taken an interest in Abi's writing.

'The 1940s. The war and just after. Not that I know much about that time.'

'Well, there's a museum in Bridport, they might have some war stuff. I could take you on my next free day, if you like?'

Abi smiled at him. 'That would be nice. Thanks.' She stood up. 'I might do some more writing now. See you later.'

'All right, who's for the pub?' asked Patrick .

'Not me,' said Carol.

'Harry?'

Carol had turned away, not wanting the others to see she was hurt. But Harry had noticed.

'That's if you don't mind, Carol?' he said.

''Not at all,' she lied.

Harry paused by her chair on the way out. 'Go up and see her. You're the grown up. It's up to you to sort things.'

'I don't know how.'

'D'you ever talk about your lives before you met Patrick?'

She shook her head. 'Abi idolised her father. If I start criticising him she'll hate me even more. She blames me for everything, then and since. Perhaps Patrick's right, she'd be happier in New York. But I'm not sure Michael would want her.'

'Harry! You coming or not?' called Jake from the hall.

'I'm coming!' Harry turned to Carol. 'Go up and talk to her. Sitting down here on your own won't change anything.'

***

'I brought you some coffee.' Carol placed the mug carefully on the table beside Abi's laptop. 'May I read what you've written?'

'There's nothing to read, I'm starting again. Different heroine. Different time.' Abi She picked up the mug and moved over to the window.

'Hmmm. Interesting. What made you choose the 1940s?'

'I don't know. It just seemed right.'

'But different. Usually you've set your stories in the same period as the house. Well, if you want more information I could try to get some books for you tomorrow. There's bound to be a good bookshop in Dorchester. Or the museum – they'll probably have something - '

'Harry's taking me to Bridport.'

'Yes, I know, but - '

'Look, Mum, I really want to get on with this.'

'Yes. Sorry.' Carol glanced around the attic. 'This looks quite nice now,' she lied. 'Shabby chic.' She wrinkled her nose. 'Funny smell, though.'

'I'm used to it – although it's kind of weird. Not dry rot - by now I know exactly how that smells.' Abi took a long sniff. 'No, this is more like - dead bodies, not that I've ever smelled a dead body, but this is how I imagine one would smell.'

Carol was shocked. 'Abi, this is silly. Why won't you

move downstairs? You'd be much more comfortable - and we - I'd like to see more of you. I don't like you being holed away up here all on your own.'

Abi's face closed. 'I've told you, I like it,' she said again. 'Anyway, you and Patrick are always busy, what difference would it make? Actually, I'd like to have my bed up here.'

'What? Certainly not! Besides, there isn't room. Desk or bed, you can't have both.' Carol sighed with frustration. 'Abi, I just want you to be happy. Patrick said – '

'What? What did Patrick say?'

'He thinks – he thinks you want to go and live with your father. And . . . if that's really what you want, Abi - '

'You want to get rid of me?'

'No, of course not, I love you – you've no idea how much.'

'Anyway, I don't want to go to Dad's. Have you been in touch with him? Did you know about his baby?'

'Baby? What baby?'

'Dad and Donna's. It's due in a few months, just like yours. So you see, I'm not wanted there either.'

'Oh, Abi!' Carol reached out her arms but Abi remained rigid in her embrace. 'Having another child doesn't mean you love your others less, or want them less. You mustn't be upset.'

'I'm not upset. It's not my business, is it? They can have a dozen babies if they want. And so can you.'

Her mother smiled. 'Not likely. But even if I could, you're my firstborn and I have a very special love for you.'

Abi moved back to her laptop. 'Thank you for the coffee, but I must get on with this.'

Carol gazed at her daughter, seeing the shuttered eyes, the tight mouth, the furrow between the brows. In her mind's eye she recalled the open, laughing, appealing little face of the ten-year-old Abi. The Abi of the old life, before Michael left them.

Suddenly she felt the weight of all the decisions she'd made since that day. Had they all been wrong? She had thought she was providing a new exciting life for all of them, with no time for regrets, for negative emotions, for loneliness, for insecurity.

She sighed and glanced at her watch. 'It's getting late, the men will be back soon. Why don't you leave your book for now?'

Abi shook her head. 'I'll give it another half hour.'

Well, it was worth another try, thought Carol as she went downstairs. But she'd have to try even harder. Abi had a stubborn streak and she was still hurting.

***

Abi had seen the disappointment on her mother's face, and the shock when she had suggested sleeping in the attic. Her mother had been right, of course. It was a horrible room. Dingy, dark, claustrophobic, way too small. Abi reckoned she could lie down twice across the room in one direction and maybe one and a half times in the

65

other. Why would she want to sleep up here? Even to spite her mother? The thought had just popped into her head from nowhere. It was a silly idea.

She stared at her laptop screen, angry and unsettled.

'Oh, dammit!'

She might as well shut down and go to bed.

As she undressed in the van she saw that she had a missed call from her Dad. Her thumb hovered for a moment over the keys and then she deleted it.

Eight

I waited all through the darkness. All I could think about was that she was writing about me, Helen. Me! We are connected and I'm overwhelmed with happiness.

She looks so tired, her eyes red-rimmed. I think she's been crying again. That woman – her mother – she's hurt her. Abi, I call, don't cry, don't be sad. I'm here and we're going to be best friends. It's a long time since I've heard my own voice. But even though I can hear it now, Abi cannot.

She's opening her box. I stand behind her. Watching. Waiting. Willing her to write my story. But where should she begin? I don't want to remember but I must.

It started when I was fourteen and my mother ran away. One Friday night she was there, kissing me goodnight, and the next morning she was gone. When she didn't return on the Saturday night my father started slamming things around, getting more and more angry.

The next Monday at school was horrible. Someone had heard about Mummy and everyone was talking about her. Miss Gordon, our headmistress, asked me if she was in hospital, but I didn't know anything and it was embarrassing. I couldn't wait to go home, hoping she would be there. But she wasn't. Not that day, nor the next day, nor any of the ones after that. A week later Daddy took me out of school and we moved to this big house in the country. Miles away. Marshbank. It had belonged to his uncle, he told me, who had died.

I didn't want to leave our old house. What if Mummy came back and I wasn't there? I didn't want to leave my school either, or my friends. Margaret Campion, Janet Fields, Patty James. We had known each other since we were five years old. I didn't want to start at a new school where I wouldn't know anyone.

'You won't be going to school,' said Daddy. 'I'm going to teach you myself.'

But Daddy wasn't a teacher. He was an accountant. And how would I make new friends if not at school? I tried to talk to him but he just shouted. His face turns dark red when he's angry, so I didn't try again .

Abi is typing so fast, as fast as I can remember what happened. Sometimes she pauses. Her brow wrinkles, she stretches her arms above her head and sighs. And then she types again.

The barrage of sound as the team ripped away panelling, clawed off window frames and set circular saws working on rafters and floorboards was constant, and it was only when it stopped for lunch that Patrick found he'd missed two calls from Carol.

'Hey, sweetheart, where are you?'

'In a cafe in Dorchester. I've been trying to get hold of you for an hour.'

'Sorry. You know what it's like when we're all working. Spent lots of money on yourself, I hope?'

'On Josh, actually. Or about to. I just thought I'd better check with you first, but we're going to have one very disappointed boy if you say no.'

'Sounds ominous. Go on, tell me what you're cooking up.'

'We got talking to a woman who finds homes for rescue dogs. She's got six at the moment, including a couple of puppies, and - well, we ended up back at her place, and Josh - he's just so excited.'

Patrick groaned. 'No, don't tell me. You've promised him a puppy. Sweetheart, it's the last thing we need here, getting in everyone's way, christening the new floors when we get them laid - '

'He's a good kid, Patrick, and he's never been any trouble. And he's never had a pet. And it won't be a puppy, more likely a full grown dog - and house trained.'

'What about Abi? Won't she be jealous?'

'I would give her anything she wants, she knows that, but now she knows about the baby, even the fact that

69

we're going to remain in this house doesn't please her.' She sighed. 'I don't know what else I can do! Anyway, what shall I tell Josh?'

'Tell him - oh, dammit, tell him OK.'

After he'd ended the call Patrick collected a can of lager from the team's portable fridge and wandered down to the old orchard. He leaned against the lichen-crusted bark of one of the apple trees and took a long slug of the cold drink. Most of the trees were dead or dying, he noticed. A job for later. Dig them all up and replace with new.

The dog would be yet another nail in his coffin. A small one, granted, compared with Carol's pregnancy and Abi's fury, but it seemed that everything now was conspiring to bury him in this one place, nice as it was, and beautiful as the house would be when he'd finished with it.

Just that morning he had received an email from his favourite estate agent, who was always looking out for suitable properties for him. He had read it so many times that he could recite the details word for word. The house was old, probably Jacobean, of timber and mellow red bricks, and it overlooked a small private lake. Like Marshbank, it stood alone, and there was no possibility of anything else being built within a mile of it. It was a wreck, but so hedged by restrictions that there were no other potential buyers and it was going for a song. But it was two hundred miles away.

While Carol was in Dorchester with Josh he had printed out the details, and now they were hidden away in the large leather case where he filed all his documents. The next step would be to go and view the house and, if it was as appealing as its photograph, to buy it. But that was impossible. The baby was due in less than five months, he had promised Carol, and Abi would hate him forever. Or would she? She might even take a grim satisfaction in the fact that he'd be letting Carol down.

***

Abi had taken a sandwich and a cup of coffee up to the attic, where the noise of the demolition below was muted.

Her new ideas for the book were going well. In her mind she had created a picture of Helen, the young girl who slept in the attic. Small and slight of build. A pale, serious face with huge shadowed eyes. Dark hair, parted in the middle and touching her narrow shoulders. How would she speak? She was no longer a servant girl, she was the daughter of the house. Who else lived there? Her father, of course. Not her mother, she would have no part in this story. Would there be others? Somehow she couldn't picture a lively, cheerful group of characters. The house itself suggested sadness, loneliness, loss. The house was as important as those who lived in it.

She had a strange sensation of being watched. Nonsense, of course. She rubbed the back of her neck, stretched, wriggled her shoulders and opened her laptop.

She was interrupted by Josh. He burst into the attic, almost falling over himself.

'Knock next time!'

71

'Mum's going to buy me a dog! And I'm allowed to choose it! We're going to bring it home tomorrow!'

Abi was furious. So they were resorting to bribes. Well, if Patrick and her Mum had any plans to bribe her, Abi, they'd be mightily disappointed.

'So? They won't let you keep it,' she said cruelly. 'Not once the baby comes.'

'What baby?'

'Mum's. They haven't told you? A baby boy. A sweet little brother for you.'

'Wow! A dog *and* a baby! Brilliant!'

'Huh! Mum and Patrick won't have time for *you* when it's born.'

'I'll have my dog.' said Josh happily.

But what will *I* have? thought Abi.

After Josh, high on excitement and anticipation, had rushed downstairs to find his mother, Abi turned back to her laptop. The familiar adrenalin of starting a new book filled her. A new world within her head, peopled with characters that she could manipulate, that might even at times manipulate her.

A world that, for a time however short, would help her to forget the frustrations of her own world.

Her phone buzzed.

'Dinner in ten minutes,' said her mother.

Always interruptions. Why couldn't they all just leave her alone? She needed to concentrate. But then her phone rang again.

'Abi, what are you doing?' snapped her mother. 'Everything's getting cold. For heaven's sake, get down here!'

Damn, damn, damn!

'All right, I'm coming!' She reached forward to close the file and it was then that she saw the words on the screen.

"I was fourteen years old when my mother ran away . . . . "

There was more. Paragraph after paragraph. But where had it come from? Abi had no recollection of typing those words – and yet how else could they have appeared on her laptop? She had that funny feeling again, of someone behind her. The nape of her neck prickled, and she turned round sharply.

'Who's there?' she asked, but of course no one answered.

Her phone rang again. She snatched it up. 'ALL RIGHT! I'M COMING!'

***

Carol had brought back several bags of goodies. Two whole cooked chickens, a mix of salads, crusty loaves, cheeses and three large ready-made trifles. Not to mention two dozen tins of pet food for tomorrow's addition to the family.

'What are we celebrating?' asked Harry as the men took their seats at the table.

'Me!' Josh shouted. 'I'm getting a dog! And Mum's getting a new baby!'

All eyes turned to Carol.

'I did wonder,' said Harry.

She nodded. 'I know. I'm putting on weight already.'

'Well, wonderful news, and congratulations!' He looked around him. 'Raise your glasses, boys! Here's to new life!'

Carol stole a glance at Abi, whose face was tight with anger. Well, there was nothing she could do or say to improve matters there.

She gazed round at the other smiling faces and raised her glass of milk.

'Boy or girl?' asked Jake.

'Boy,' said Patrick, 'but we'll have to wait a few years before he can join the team.'

Abi stood up, pushing her plate away so violently that her glass of fruit juice tipped over. And then she was gone.

Harry looked after her, shaking his head.

'That one,' he said slowly. 'She needs a bit of TLC.'

'I know,' said Carol. 'But she won't accept it.'

The jokes and the laughter were gone. The men ate their chicken and salads in silence.

'Why does she have to spoil everything?' Patrick whispered to Carol.

'I'll talk to her again in the morning,' Carol promised.

But the mood around the table lightened when Josh rushed out to the kitchen and returned with a can of dog meat and a tin opener,

'Can I open this?'

'What? You'd rather eat that than chicken and trifle?' teased Patrick.

'I just want to taste it - and smell it.'

They all watched as Josh took a mouthful of the dark glutinous contents and then spat it out all over his plate of chicken.

'Aagh! Yuk! That's disgusting!'

Nine

I am in her head! I am overwhelmed with happiness and love, yes, love. Abi, my friend, is writing my story. I can share with her everything that happened to me in this house. No one else may ever read her words – our words – but I don't care. It's enough that she is here to share my memories.

Sometimes, if she's away from the attic for too long, I steel myself to follow her around the house. Wherever I go I see men, hammering and sawing and mixing things in buckets. Their voices are loud like his, they shout to each other. There are other noises too, music that seems very fierce, tools that they plug into the walls and that scream and whine.

The men frighten me. I keep my distance, but what if one – or all of them – could see me? I think I am invisible, but how can I be sure of that? If they saw me, would they run away? Or would they chase me? Try to destroy me?

I wish, I wish Abi could move into the attic, be there night and day, with me. And I wish I could keep all those other people away. The noisy men and the boy. And the pregnant woman, Abi's mother. All I want is Abi.

Back in the attic Abi burned with embarrassment, desperate to forget the scene downstairs. Her friends, Harry, Jake, Brandon, Marek. She had seen the looks they gave each other as she rushed out of the room. She had to learn to hide her feelings, but it was hard when she had this great lump of hatred and resentment inside her. She ached, actually ached, with it.

She opened her laptop and stared at the screen, a blank space waiting to be filled with words. The book. Her refuge. Her escape. But how could she write now? *What could she write?*

Mothers. Perhaps she would give Helen a mother as selfish and heartless as her own, put all her anger and frustration into Helen's story. She rubbed the tears from her eyes and began to type.

"I missed my mother. How long is it since she went away? Every day I try to picture her, worried that my memories are fading.

She was small, lots smaller than the other mothers. And very beautiful. She was like a beautiful fairy without wings. She had long golden hair and she would tie it all up on top with a big blue bow. She tied mine up the same, only with a white bow.

She laughed a lot and we played lots of games. Sometimes we were still playing games when Daddy came home from work and he'd be angry because there was no tea ready. Or she'd put something on the stove to cook and then she'd put a record on the record player and grab my hands and we'd waltz all over the house. So fast sometimes it was like flying.

And then the stuff in the pan would burn and the bottom of the pan would be all brown, so she'd take it outside to the garden and hide it under the hedge with the others. Daddy would get really mad then.

'Don't you know there's a war on, woman?' he'd shout. 'Where are the coupons coming from to buy more food? And new pans, when they're all being melted down to make planes?'

And he'd hunt out the burnt pans from under the hedge and make her scrub them all with wire wool until her fingers were raw and red but the pans were clean again.

Why did she leave me?"

Abi leaned back and read the words on the screen. Read them as if they were a page from someone else's novel. These were not the words she had intended to write, and there had been none of her usual labouring to find the right phrases, the right emotions.

She hadn't noticed the change of temperature, not until she closed down her laptop. It was no more than a slight change in the atmosphere, a coolness, the tiniest sighing movement of air, but she shivered and the back of her neck began to tingle. She had that strange feeling again, that someone was standing behind her chair, watching her. She turned her head slowly. Of course, no one was there. All the same, she didn't want to stay any longer. She stood up in a hurry, wanting to rush downstairs, back to other people, however little they cared for her.

'Don't go.' The voice was in her head. At least, she thought so.

'Please don't go.'

78

She almost knocked her laptop to the floor as she turned around. There was no one else in the room, of course there wasn't. Unless it was a ghost and she didn't believe in ghosts.

At the door she peered back into the corners of the attic. Nothing there, except a few more dead flies, and a spider in the corner of the window, busily strengthening its web.

Downstairs Abi found Patrick in the room he and Carol had designated as an office. He was rooting through a stack of papers. His face flushed when he saw her. What was he up to?

'Hi,' he said,. 'Your Mum and Josh have gone to pick up the dog.' He stuffed the papers back into his leather case. 'God knows what he'll come home with!'

Abi shrugged. 'Who cares? As long as he keeps it out of my way.'

'Shit, Abi, just listen to yourself! You may be angry with me and your Mum, but what's Josh done to you? He's your kid brother and he worships you. He deserves a dog, he's a good kid.'

'Not like me, yeah?'

'Exactly!'

Abi flushed. 'Well, he may not be such a good kid when the baby arrives and Mum loses interest in both of us.'

'You're so screwed up. The baby will never displace you – or Josh. Your Mum loves you both, and this house is for you too, not just for us. We thought you were OK with it.'

'Well, you thought wrong,' she flung at him, 'and the

79

sooner I get away from you both, the happier I'll be!' Her eyes hot with tears, she turned away from him.

He caught her arm.

'Wait! OK, I know you still love your Dad and you think I'm a pretty lousy substitute, so what do you really want to do? Josh said you were saving up to fly to New York. Is that right?'

She said nothing.

'Abi, if you really are planning to go live with your Dad, I'll talk to your Mum. She'll be upset but I'm sure - '

'I can't go to New York. Not now. Donna's pregnant too.'

Patrick's eyes widened. 'Oh. Does your Mum know?'

'I told her.'

'And how did she take it?'

Abi shrugged. ''All right, I suppose. Why should she care? She was glad to get rid of him.'

Patrick shook his head. 'I don't think it was quite like that.' He snapped shut the fasteners on his case. 'Well, better get on. I'm supposed to be chasing some deliveries.'

As Abi was leaving, he called her back. 'Go easy on her.'

She nodded. Still angry but ashamed as well, she escaped into the garden. All she seemed to do nowadays was lash out at people.

In the centre of what had once been a lawn a bonfire smouldered, waiting to be fed again. It had been lit as soon as the team started stripping out the old worm-infested woodwork.

She wandered down to the orchard, as far as she could get from the house. The grass was long and wrapped itself around her legs. The garden dozed. The birds were silent, stupefied by the August heat. Only the pigeons on their endless search for food broke the silence.

'It's cold, it is. It's cold, it is.'

Stupid pigeons! Couldn't even get the seasons right.

There were a few apples on the trees. She pulled one, wondering if it was edible, but it was wrinkled and scabby. She tossed it aside and went back to her attic. At least there she could forget everything that was going on in the house below her, and concentrate on her book.

***

It was mid-afternoon when Carol and Josh returned. The men had moved into the garden with mugs of tea and a pack of jam doughnuts.

Josh was wild with excitement, proudly clutching a chain leading to a very large and hairy hound.

'This is my dog! Mine!'

Marek put down his mug.

'Is very big!'

Carol laughed. 'He wouldn't have any of the smaller ones. As soon as he set eyes on this one, that was it. True love!'

Harry smiled. 'It looks as if it's been knitted. Badly, at that.'

'Well, at least he might put off any burglars who come sneaking around,' said Jake.

'Doubt it,' said Carol. 'Apparently he's a real coward.

Scared of shadows, cars, loud noises, cats – you name it!'

'What's his name?' asked Harry.

'Dog!'

'Aren't you going to give him a proper name?'

'That *is* his proper name. Dog. With a capital D,' said Josh. 'I named him.'

'Clever. Just hope there won't be any other dogs around when you call him.'

'There aren't any other dogs.' Josh turned to Carol. 'D'you think he'll get lonely?'

'Not with you to take care of him.'

'I'm going to show Abi!'

'Best wait till she comes down,' warned Carol, knowing he and the dog would get a cold reception, but Josh couldn't wait. He was already through the door and urging Dog up the stairs, the chain clattering on each step, the dog panting behind him.

***

'Knock!' yelled Abi, but too late. Josh was already there, something huge and heavy footed beside him.

'This is Dog,' said Josh proudly. 'Isn't he lovely? I asked Mum if we could have him in the Hymer tonight because he'll probably feel lonely and scared, but she said he's too big. So-o-oo, I'm going to sleep in the house with him! In a sleeping bag! Brandon's coming too and we're going to have a midnight feast! You can come, if you like, Abi.'

'No, thank you.'

Josh's face fell. 'Don't you like him, Abi?'

She stared at the dog. She thought he was probably the ugliest animal she'd ever seen. But if Josh liked him . . .

'He's all right, I suppose.' But was he? The dog was holding back, cowering against the doorway, making whimpering noises.

'What's the matter, Dog?' said Josh. 'What can you see? Sit!"

But Dog didn't sit. Instead, ears flattened, eyes protruding, he rushed at the corner of the attic, his barks rising in volume, And then he lifted his head and let out a long howl.

'For Heaven's sake, Josh, get him out of here!'

It took both of them to tug and shove Dog out of the room, but once outside his howls diminished to a low whimper.

'Don't bring him up here again!' Abi snapped as she slammed the door shut.

She wondered what could have upset the crazy animal. She stared around her. But all she could see was the resident spider, comatose in its web.

She recalled her own sensation of being watched. But that was nonsense. The attic was just another room, albeit a small one. Perhaps Dog's previous owner had kept him in a very small space. She shrugged. There was nothing she could do about it. She supposed most rescue dogs had hang-ups. She hoped Josh would be able to sort out Dog's, but if past memories kept him out of the attic, that suited her just fine.

Ten

I used to like dogs. Once I would have been so pleased to have the company of one. It would have comforted me in the loneliness of the silent days and nights. But the boy's dog, such a huge, ugly animal, was frightening, until I realised that it was more frightened of me!

Question: If animals and birds can see me, why can't humans? Why can't Abi? Are human brains so tightly packed with facts and thoughts and memories that they only register what they have been taught to see? If someone came to my attic who believed in ghosts, would that person see me? And if so, when Abi has finished recording my story and knows what happened to me, would she then see me?

Perhaps in time, if I really concentrate and if I can keep everyone else out of my attic, perhaps it will happen. Already I am in her head.

Dinner was a quiet meal. Abi had heard some conversation as she came down the stairs but it ceased when she entered the room. They're all beginning to hate me, she thought. But none of this was her fault, was it? It was them. The family. People who are supposed to care about you. They're the ones who make you behave badly. They take you away and you never again see the people you've left behind. Like Tim. Or *they* go away, like my Dad. And now he and Donna are starting a new family and I may never see him again either.

Tim. Oh, Tim! He hadn't called her again. She had several times picked up her phone to call him, but pride had told her that it would be a wasted effort. There were too many miles between them now.

But she shouldn't be taking it out on Josh. None of this was his fault. His face was tear stained and the food on his plate was untouched.

'I'm sorry about your dog,' she said.

'He won't even go up the stairs now! You frightened him.'

'I didn't!' But something had.

'Maybe we can try again tomorrow,' she said.' We'll take him up between us.'

Josh brightened. 'Promise?'

'Promise.'

Later she regretted her promise. Did she really want to allow Josh and his huge monster dog into her private sanctuary? No. But nor did she want Josh's misery on her conscience.

She glanced at the other faces around the table. Harry, everyone's rock, the oldest in Patrick's team. She knew she'd disappointed him recently. She regretted that. Jake, who had been a friend of Patrick's own father and in his spare time played the fiddle to entertain the others.

85

Brandon, the nearest in age to herself, her closest friend within the team. And Marek, who had been with them for eighteen months now. Sad faced Marek, missing the family he had left behind in Bulgaria.

She risked alienating them all. Is that really what she wanted? Her fight was with her mother and Patrick, not them.

She sat up straight, painted a smile on her face.

'So, are we going to the pub tonight? Is anyone going to treat me to a lemonade?'

***

The next morning, after breakfast she and Josh put Dog on his chain and started to coax him up the stairs. He trotted willingly enough across the hall, his huge paws thudding on the worn parquet floor, but when they reached the stairs he began to whimper.

'Come on, Dog,' urged Josh. 'No one's going to hurt you. I'll look after you.'

He was a big animal and resisted all the way as they dragged and pushed him, step after step, up the stairs. They managed to get him as far as the first floor landing but once there he sat back on his haunches and the howls began.

'What's up with him?' asked Patrick, opening the door of one of the bedrooms and releasing a cloud of old plaster particles.

'He doesn't want to go up to Abi's attic,' said Josh.

'Not surprised.' Patrick glanced at Abi. 'No one with any sense would want to go in there.'

Abi ignored him. She looked down at Dog. Hunched

and cowering, ears flattened, his eyes beseeched her, begging her to protect him. But from what?

She sighed. 'We'll have to let him go, Josh. Sorry.'

After the dog, with Josh in pursuit, had scampered down the stairs, almost falling over itself in its flight, she searched the corners of the attic again but could see nothing to upset the stupid animal. All was calm, silent, peaceful.

And her laptop awaited her.

What would she write today? She had no idea, and that made it even more exciting than usual.

She sat down and switched on.

Reading through the pages she had keyed in yesterday she marvelled again. She still had no idea where all of it was coming from. It was almost as if someone else was dictating to her, but that was impossible. Clearly her subconscious was dredging up a mix of fact, fiction and fantasy and was spewing it out through the forefront of her brain.

***

Helen and her father were now in the kitchen – the kitchen here in Marshbank, with the cream and green cupboards and the old oak table, which probably was not as battered and stained then. They were eating lunch. A scanty meal because there would be rationing.

Helen's father was reading a newspaper. It was three days old, Helen noticed, and the news was all about the War. Helen had a book of poetry by Percy Bysshe Shelley propped up against the teapot. The book had belonged to her mother, one of the few that had been brought with their belongings to Marshbank. Her father snatched it from her.

"'What's this rubbish?'

'Poetry. Miss Harding was teaching us, and Mummy bought the book for me. It's lovely. Mummy and I - '

'Well, you don't need poetry now,' he said, and he threw the book in the kitchen bin.

'You said you were going to teach me,' I whispered, 'but you're not teaching me anything, not even maths. How can I learn if no one teaches me? '

'Dammit, girl, when have I got time? And what does it matter while we're at war? There's more important things to worry about.'

I straightened up. He was so angry all the time, and he was drinking a lot. Whisky. I don't know where he was getting it, but while we might not have any bread or butter or meat, there was always whisky.

'You should have time. You don't go to work now. And where's Mummy?' My voice trembled. 'I want Mummy. Where is she? Why isn't she here?'

He stared at me for a long moment and then he stood up, his chair falling over behind him.

That was the first time he hit me.

After he'd gone out I rescued Percy Bysshe Shelley from the bin, collected all Mummy's other books from the study, and took them up to my bedroom. I hid them in the gap between the base of my wardrobe and the floor, and hoped Daddy would be too drunk to remember them."

A knock on the attic door brought Ali back. She

frowned. Her mother. Bound to be.

'I'm busy. Go away.'

A second knock, more tentative. Not her mother then. She would have barged in, determined once more to 'make amends' and Abi would have told her once more, 'Too late.'

'Who is it?' she called.

'Marek. Can I speak with you?''

Marek? What could he want? She had barely spoken to him since he joined the team. There was the language problem, of course. He knew no English on his arrival and was a slow learner. Apart from the other team members he had no friends that she knew of. She closed her laptop and turned around.

'Come in.'

He was holding a piece of paper and handed it to her. 'You write book? I write poem.'

Yes, it looked like a poem. Handwritten, divided into four-line verses. But all in Bulgarian.

'I'm sorry, I can't read it. But poetry! That's amazing.'

'About my family. My wife, Elena. My daughter, Petya. They still in Bulgaria. I send them poems.'

'You miss them.'

'Yes. I see them two, three times a year.' He smiled, the smile lifting the contours of his usually mournful face. 'Elena, new baby coming December.'

Abi sighed. Babies. The last thing she wanted to hear about.

'Congratulations.'

'Your mother. Baby should make her happy. Make you happy too. Babies God's gift.'

Abi closed her eyes. 'This isn't your business, Marek. It's private.'

'I worry for you. I not like see you unhappy. Angry. Families must – glue? - stick? - together. Very important.'

'Well, thank you for caring, Marek, but I can handle it. Now you should go. Patrick will be missing you.' She handed the piece of paper back to him. 'And thank you for showing me your poem.'

He took the paper, refolded it carefully and put it in his pocket. He nodded at the laptop.

'Back with your book,' he said. 'To write, it helps, yes?'

She nodded. 'It does.'

He turned to go. He had taken only one step when there was a harsh splintering noise. One of the old floorboards had given way, taking with it Marek's right leg up to the calf.

'Oh my God! Are you all right?' Abi rushed to help him.

Marek groaned as she tried to pull him clear. 'No! It hurts. Get Patrick. Please!'

As Abi rushed down the stairs Patrick appeared from one of the bedrooms.

'What's going on?''

'It's Marek. A floorboard gave way and his leg's bleeding!'

Within a minute the whole team was crowding into the

tiny attic.

'No! Get out, the rest of the boards are probably rotten. You too, Abi,' said Patrick. 'Harry, just you – and bring a saw and a crowbar.'

Abi hovered in the doorway as the two men carefully removed the boards that surrounded Marek.

'Looks bad,' said Patrick when they had freed his leg. 'Scraped down to the bone, bleeding quite a lot. Marek, we'll have to get that seen to and you'll probably need a tetanus jab. Filthy down there. Harry, can you drive Marek?'

He looked round for Abi. 'Well, that's it. Get your laptop and stuff. No way you can work in here now. Your Mum will sort something for you downstairs.'

'No! I want to stay here,' Abi protested. 'I'll be careful.'

But Patrick was shaking his head.

'Out of bounds. Unsafe.'

'Can't you get Brandon to put a couple of new boards in?'

'The whole floor needs replacing, probably the other attics too. And it's not a priority job. Sorry, Abi.' Patrick smiled. She didn't smile back.

Stomping into the attic, making the old boards creak ominously, she grabbed her laptop and files.

Damn Marek. This was all his fault.

Eleven

I am not a bad person. I just wanted to frighten him, keep him away from my attic and Abi. I don't want to think about him hurting, but it was his own fault. He should have stayed downstairs.

Now I am angry with myself. In getting rid of the man I've also got rid of Abi. Oh yes, I can follow her downstairs but I want her here, in my space, just the two of us alone together. I was stupid, stupid.

Yet a part of me feels triumphant. Of course I knew the floorboards were loose in that spot but I had never before considered I might have the power to make things happen. To direct people - living people – by my will.

After he'd scribbled a notice for the attic door warning everyone to keep out, Patrick suddenly remembered that downstairs he'd left his leather case open. He had been re-reading the details of the Jacobean property when Abi called him and he was pretty sure he'd left them in full view. He hurried to hide them away but was too late.

'What's this?' White faced, Carol stood by the case, the file crushed to a lumpen ball. She threw the ball at him. It missed and rolled across the floor.

'Nothing. It just came in the post.'

'When?' Her voice was sharp.

'A couple of weeks ago.'

'So why do you still have it? And why did you hide it?' She glared at him. 'You're not seriously considering it? Going off to Norfolk, leaving us here? Or uprooting us all again, turning Abi *completely* against me?'

'No, no! It was just - maybe it'll still be available later on - when the baby's born, when - '

'I've told you, Patrick, I'm not moving again.'

'You've always loved it - the excitement — some place new to work your magic on - you and me, the best team in the - '

'That was before, Patrick.' Her hand came to her stomach in a protective gesture. 'Don't you want this baby?'

'Yes, of course I do. It's just - ' He stared out of the window. The sky was thick with rain, the old apple trees in the orchard bowed down with it. 'It's just — it's hard to change, Carol. I don't know if I *can* change.'

'So . . . What's the alternative? Splitting up?'

'God, no! Never that!' He was horrified. 'Never!'

'Well, you'll just have to think of a solution then, won't you? Because I can't.'

After she had stamped from the room he picked up the property details and tenderly smoothed them out.

Had he lied to Carol? Did he really want this baby? Now? When the business was going so well? Carol's pregnancy, which should have brought them closer together, was creating a deepening chasm between them. As for their romantic partnership, that was beginning to lose its colour. Carol's physical attractions, the house and the investments that her guilt-ridden husband had left her, plus her considerable talents as an interior designer, had been a magnet that had pulled him in.

Briefly he considered the consequences of splitting up. There would be no marriage complications. His Catholic upbringing had been watered down considerably over the years but it still proved useful.

On the other hand, had they married he would now be able to claim a considerable portion of their capital, regardless of who had provided it initially. Without that deep well of money to draw on he would have to take several steps down the ladder, and he was not prepared to do that.

Shit! He was caught. First, the baby. Then the ultimatum. Even the house was fighting him. There were far more problems than he'd anticipated. It was all going to take longer than he had planned. He was trapped. No longer free to do exactly as he wanted. Might as well propose and be damned!

***

Harry came back just before lunch.

'Marek's still waiting for an X-ray,' he told Patrick. 'I bought him some sandwiches, but I thought I'd better get back here. I'll call the Unit later and go back for him.' He stared at Patrick. 'You're looking a bit long in the face. What's up?

'I'm in the doghouse.'

'Oh? She'll come round. She's not a bad kid really.'

'No, not Abi. It's Carol. She found details of a property I'd been looking at and now she won't speak to me.' Patrick took the file out of his case and showed it to Harry.

Harry read through the details slowly and carefully. 'I can see why you're nursing this. It's pretty special, isn't it? And you don't think she'll budge?'

'It's the baby. The honeymoon period's well and truly over, Harry. Carol just wants to settle down, do all the things expectant mothers do, but it's not me, is it? I can't see myself stagnating in Dorset for the next five or ten years. Going to church on Sundays, joining Rotary, going to the same pub every Saturday night. Wearing a suit. And then there's you and the rest of the team. How would we make a living?'

He glanced at Harry, suddenly anxious. 'Unless, of course, you'd want to move on?'

'Not me,' said Harry. 'Dunno about the others.'

'So what d'you think I should do?'

Harry was silent for so long that Patrick thought he wasn't going to answer.

Then, 'I think you'll have to give it up. There'll be others. Just wait and see,' he said. 'The baby will be here before

95

this place is ready for sale and Carol might feel different after that.'

Patrick sighed. 'I doubt it.'

* * *

Carol was missing at lunch, which made Patrick apprehensive. Was this going to be a cold war, he wondered? But when he went searching, he found her in one of the first floor bedrooms overlooking the sea. She was up on a ladder hanging a pair of blue linen curtains at the window.

Her body, stretched to hook the fabric to a brass rod, was no longer slender and shapely. Her bulge was quite prominent now and her legs, bare below a pair of cut-offs, were sturdy and blue-veined. Her features seemed heavier too – and was that the beginning of a double chin?

He glanced away. He had made his bed, and if it was now showing its rumples and creases, so be it.

'I found these in Dorchester,' she said. 'Nice, aren't they? I thought they might make this room more acceptable for Abi.'

'You shouldn't be up there,' he scolded her, but he was relieved that the anger had disappeared from her voice. He caught her around the hips and lifted her from the ladder. 'I'll do it.'

'I'm only fourteen weeks. When I'm nearer term and I'm carrying all before me I'll be more careful.'

'Are we OK?' he asked, holding her to him.

She reached up and kissed him. 'I can't stay angry with you for long.'

96

'Thank goodness!'

'Where *is* Abi? Did she turn up for lunch?'

He nodded. 'She was there when I left.'

***

But Abi had not stayed long at the table. As soon as Patrick left the room she pushed her plate aside and headed for the stairs.

The door of the little attic had not been barred. She turned the knob and slipped inside. She thought of Marek and the scream that had been torn from him when the broken boards savaged his leg. Poor Marek.

Patrick and Harry had enlarged the hole in the floor considerably, in order to pull Marek free. She squatted down and tested the boards with her hands, hoping she could still persuade Patrick to make a temporary repair.

It was then that she saw something in the space beneath the boards, a pale glimmer against dark shadow. She lay down, inserting an arm into the cavity, scrabbling through the thick clinging dust. She took an intake of breath when she saw what she had rescued.

Outside the room she heard footsteps. Tucking her find, filthy as it was, beneath the belt line of her jeans, she put a finger to her lips as Harry entered the room.

'I know, I know, I'm not supposed to be here. Sorry!'

Harry sighed. 'Go on, then. But stay away until we've made the place safe. You saw what happened to Marek!'

'Promise! '

Downstairs she hurried out to the Hymer. Once inside and with the door locked she brushed the dust of years from the book's leather cover. It was a diary. And the

97

date? 1940. But whose was it? With trembling fingers she began to turn the fragile pages.

There were two styles of handwriting. One a strong, sloping scrawl, the entries brief and in ink, just a record of appointments. But alongside and filling all the gaps there were entries in another hand. The pages were yellowed and filthy and the script was tiny and crabbed, written in pencil that was barely legible now. It was difficult to pick out individual words and some of the pages had clearly formed lunch or dinner for mice.

She turned back to the beginning and the entries written in the stronger hand. She had read no more than three or four pages before she saw the name. Helen! Appointments with Helen's doctor. Her teacher. Shopping with Helen for new shoes.

Abi sat back on her heels and stared at the diary. This was authentication. Helen had been a real person, a person who existed in the 1940s. She was not just a spark in Abi's imagination.

She fetched the magnifying glass that her mother kept in one of the cupboards. An hour passed before she could make any sense of Helen's pencilled notes but even as she turned the fragile pages they began to tell a story. Helen's story.

The diary was so old, so damaged. Already, even with Abi's careful handling, many of the pages were crumbling. She would have to transfer the notes on to her laptop as soon as possible.

Handling the little book as delicately as she could, she hid it in the bottom of her drawer and rushed back to the house.

'Where's my laptop?' she demanded of Patrick.

'Your Mum's put it in your new room. First floor front!' he shouted after her as she ran, two at a time, up the stairs.

'I want my laptop!' she shouted to her mother, who was filling a vase with flowers.

'It's here. All ready for you. What d'you think of your new room? I bought the curtains and cushions in your favourite colours, and you've got much more light in here – oh, and you can have the lamp from - '

Abi glanced round carelessly. 'It's OK, but I need my laptop. I'm going to work in the Hymer.'

She grabbed the laptop, and ran.

***

My father was pacing the floor and raging. I couldn't believe what he was telling me, that my mother cared nothing for me.

"She's abandoned us," he told me. "Gone off with her fancy man, forgotten all about you. You think she loved you? She didn't care tuppence for either of us."

"She did, she did! She loved me, I know she did. She'll come back, Daddy, I know it. Perhaps when the war's over - "

Abi paused and stared at the screen. She realised she had been holding her breath as she typed Helen's words. Words that had been scribbled more than seventy years ago.

Her phone rang. She ignored it.

"She'll never come back. She's with him, and good riddance!" He stared at me, putting his face close to mine

so I could see the flushed veins on his nose and cheeks, breathe in the smell of the whisky that he has started to drink all through the day and the evening. He has no job now and he rarely goes out, except to buy more whisky and a few scraps of food.

I don't know when I feel worst. When he is home, shouting and glaring at me, or when he locks me up in this tiny attic and goes out. Some nights I think he goes to one of the local pubs and doesn't come back for hours.

"And you know what makes me really angry?"

I shook my head and backed away.

"That she left you behind. You, who aren't even my daughter. You're his brat but now I'm supposed to look after you."

He slammed his hand down on the kitchen table, so hard that all the dishes rattled and the knives and forks clattered and the milk, sour from two days ago, slopped over the rim of the jug.

That night he locked me in the attic again. I hoped he was going to come back when he calmed down. I hadn't had any tea, and it was getting dark. There is no electric light and I don't like the dark, especially up here where I can hear the scurry of mice or rats in the rafters and behind the walls. There is no bed either. Just an old chair and a rickety table covered by a moth eaten crimson plush tablecloth.

The hours passed. Outside I heard the hoot of an owl down in the orchard, and somewhere the shrill bark of a fox. Faintly I heard the chimes of the hall clock. Midnight. Daddy wasn't coming now.

No, not Daddy. But what should I call him? This man who said he was not my father?

It grew colder. I pulled the cloth off the table, wrapped it around me and curled up on the floor. But the attic was growing light again before I slept.

I awoke to sunlight streaming through the tiny window. The sun was high in the sky. That meant it was mid-morning at least. I had eaten nothing since lunch the previous day, and then only the crust off a stale loaf and a couple of apples from the orchard. Was he going to let me out so I could have breakfast? Or was it too late? Had he already gone out? My stomach was an empty cavern, and it was beginning to hurt.

In a panic now, I hammered on the door. 'Daddy! Daddy!' I shouted. But only silence answered me.

It was another two hours or more before he released me.

As she finished typing Abi became aware that someone was hammering on the Hymer door, and then banging on the window.

'Abi, it's dinner time. Mum sent me for you.'

'Tell her I'm not hungry,'

'She said you'd say that, and I'm to fetch you anyway,' shouted Josh.

Abi frowned. 'Five minutes, tell her.'

But it was nearer fifteen when she finally closed her laptop and hid the diary, now carefully wrapped inside a silk scarf that her mother had given her, beneath the other clothes in her drawer.

Twelve

The diaries! I am so glad Abi has found one of them. Now she will be able to go on with our book.

I want to spend more time with her, standing at her shoulder as she writes. But she has given in and is using the new room her mother has prepared for her. I want to help Abi but I can't concentrate when that woman is there. The little house on wheels was better but to get there I have to pass through so many rooms, and then the garden, with all its memories.

I go back to my attic and find two of the men measuring the floor. I don't want to go in but I hover outside the door, listening to their conversation. They are planning to take up all the floorboards and replace them with new. But my other diary is still beneath those boards. Abi must find it before they start their repairs!

I know where I hid it. I just have to make sure she

knows too.

Reluctantly, under pressure from both her mother and Patrick, Abi was back in her new writing space – The Blue Room, Carol had christened it - but although the urge to write was as strong as ever, she couldn't concentrate. She had spent the last hour staring at the blank screen of her laptop while Carol hovered in the doorway.

'You do like it, don't you, Abi?'

'Go *away*!' Abi muttered under her breath.

She hadn't brought the diary with her, and now she was wondering how she had managed to start the story, anyway? There was no doubt that everything she had written before was about a girl called Helen. And now she had proof that there had been a real Helen, here in this house. Surely that went beyond mere coincidence. Abi didn't believe in ghosts, but perhaps something of that poor girl, some relic, some memory, some pocket of energy, still lived on in Marshbank. And if it was true, was Helen using Abi to tell her story? The possibility was both scary and exciting.

But the screen remained blank. She needed the diary. And what if there were more diaries?

The men hadn't started repairs yet, and they were all out in the garden, swilling tea, Marek and Brandon smoking.

'I'm just going to get a drink,' she told her mother, but outside on the landing she crept up the stairs.

In the attic she tiptoed over the floor, inspecting it inch

103

by inch. Where should she start?

'Help me!' she said out loud. And it was as if Helen heard her. Abi found herself moving towards the far left corner of the room. Squatting down, she saw that two of the boards were slightly raised. She clawed at them, breaking a fingernail, but they came up quite easily.

And there she found another small book.

'Got you!' she whispered.

'You're not supposed to be up here.' Josh was standing in the doorway, his voice accusing.

'Neither are you.'

'What are you doing?'

'Nothing. I was just tidying up.'

He looked at her, disbelieving. 'You never tidy up.'

'You're such a pain, Josh. Go away!'

He stared at her. 'You never do anything with me any more.' His voice trembled.

He was right, Abi realised. Too bound up in her own sense of injury, she had neglected him for weeks. I'm a horrible person, she reproached herself.

'I'm sorry. Look, I just need to go back to the Hymer, and then maybe we could go for a walk. Take your monster dog?'

'Really?' Josh's eyes lit up.'Wow! I'll go and get him ready!'

After she had hidden the diary with the earlier one, she met Josh at the front door. Even then, Dog's ears flattened and his gaze flickered from Abi to the staircase.

'Come on,' she said to Josh. 'Let's take him outside. Got a ball? No? OK, A stick will do.'

And for the next hour they played the age-old game of fetch-and-carry until Abi was bored to her limit, longing to get back to her writing. But Josh was so happy, so delighted to have her company that she delayed returning for another half an hour.

'That was great,' said Josh as they walked back. 'Absolutely fantabulous!'

She glanced down at him.

She was not the only member of the family to feel lonely and neglected, she realised. Josh always made the best of everything, extracting pleasure from the smallest activities, but it was a solitary life for him too, with Mum and Patrick absorbed throughout the day and most of the evenings with their plans, and the men taking few breaks between their various tasks. Even Harry, Josh's hero, had little time to spare for him. But when had she ever heard Josh complain?

'We'll do this again tomorrow,' she said.

'Really? Wow!' Josh leapt in the air, his face flushed with delight.

Even Dog looked pleased, ears pricked, tail erect, almost a smile on his hairy face.

Until they reached the front door of Marshbank. And then he backed away, his tail disappearing between his legs. He whimpered quietly.

'Dog! Don't be silly,' said Josh as he tried to drag the cowed animal over the threshold. 'What's wrong with him?' he asked Abi.

'I don't know,' said Abi. But she did know.

***

Back in the Blue Room Abi opened her laptop, a bubble of excitement catching her breath. What would she – and Helen – write next? The diaries lay beside her, full of secrets, full of Helen's life. She opened the first one and turned to the page she had marked.

And there was her mother, once again standing in the doorway. 'How's it going?'

Abi shoved the diaries into her folder. 'It isn't!'

'Oh. Can I help? Are you sure you wouldn't like me to read what you've written so far? You used to let me help.'

'No' Abi took a deep breath. 'It's just – I can't concentrate here, I need to be in the attic.'

'But that's silly.' Carol's face crumpled. 'This room's so much nicer. And – I'll try to keep out of your way.'

'It's not you,' Abi lied. 'I just – I can't write anywhere else.'

'Well . . . I don't understand, but I'll see what I can do. Perhaps Patrick can reschedule some of the work, although he won't be happy about it.'

No, he won't, Abi thought to herself. Patrick never liked anything to interfere with his schedule. He would put forward reasons, good reasons, to support his refusal. But surely he'd prefer her to be tucked away in the attic, out of sight, out of mind?

In the early days when he had first courted her mother he had charmed her, going out of his way to play games with her, to make her laugh. He had bought her a doll, a doll with long fair hair like her own, and he had told her and Josh tales about his Romany grandmother who lived in a painted caravan and had four children and made medicines out of herbs.

But now, if Abi's mother wasn't around, he scarcely bothered to hide his irritation, his impatience with her. Abi supposed it was natural enough. If someone didn't like you, or resented you, or hated what you were doing, how could you go on liking that person? Unless you were a saint, and Patrick was no saint. He could be a hard man, working his team for long hours and accepting no excuses, not even from poor Marek whose leg was taking a long time to heal. She suspected too that he wasn't particularly loyal to Carol. Several times on the team's visits to the local pub (without Carol, who lately found the aromas of stale beer and chips upsetting) Abi had seen him chatting up the barmaid.

'Maybe I'll just work in the van.' She turned away from her mother's sad eyes.

But when Carol had gone back to her office Abi crept

up the stairs to the attic. Closing the door behind her, she moved carefully around the edges of the room to sit cross legged beneath the window, her laptop open on her knees.

She was edgy, irritable, even remorseful, although not too much. She owed nothing to her mother, she told herself. Mothers were supposed to put their children first, she reminded herself, and when did Carol ever do that? But she didn't want to think about her mother now.

After a few moments absorbing the silent dust-laden atmosphere of the attic she took out the diaries, opened her laptop and laid her fingers on the keys.

The writing helps to make the days more bearable, although I have to listen for his footsteps and hide my notes before he unlocks the door.

I couldn't go on calling him Daddy. Once or twice I had forgotten and he was furious. "I told you, I'm not your Daddy." So I decided not to call him anything. But when I started writing these notes i had to call him something and I decided on a new name. The Beast. Because that's what he is. A cruel, horrible, nasty beast, and I'm glad he's not my father!

I'm so scared. Scared and hungry.

At night I cry for my mother. Please come back, I pray, even though I hate her now.

Mothers are supposed to put their children first, aren't they? Not abandon them, run away with other men. I don't blame her for leaving The Beast, but how could she

108

leave me? Without a word, without even a goodbye kiss. I can never forgive her. Never.

I am so lonely. I have no friends. I have nothing. I see no one except him. And I am so scared. It's rare now for him to let me out of the attic. He doesn't want to see me. One day he may lock me in and forget all about me forever. That is my greatest fear.

I cannot escape. When I am released from the attic he is always somewhere close. No one visits. No one telephones. No tradesmen call. I pray that one day he may get drunk before he goes out and so forget to lock me in, but I don't really expect God to answer me.

At night in the dark I hear the drone of planes above my head, often seeming low enough to scrape the roof of the attic. Are they British planes? Or German bombers? I can only guess. The Beast never speaks to me. I have no way of knowing if we are winning or losing the war but it seems to have gone on forever.

Sometimes lately, although the planes frighten me, I almost wish that a bomb would fall directly on this house. Kill him. Kill me. What have I got to live for? My mother is gone, there is no real hope of her coming back. No hope of him releasing me.

Which would be worse? To slowly starve to death here? Or to experience the sudden instantaneous blast of a German bomb and know no more?

Abi sat back and re-read the words on the screen. Her fingers trembled, her shoulders ached and her eyes were blurred and swollen, as if she had cried a torrent of tears.

Copying Helen's own words it was as though she herself was reliving Helen's nightmare.

She saved the file and closed her laptop.

Thirteen

The men have come to repair the floor. They are taking far too long, and I know I won't see Abi here again until they finish. I watch from the doorway. I suppose I am curious. I know so little about men, except that they frighten me. Perhaps they are not all like The Beast, but even so, I am glad they cannot see me.

The one they call Marek, the one whose leg I hurt, is with them. I don't look at him.

I wish they would hurry, go away, but they are laughing and joking, smoking cigarettes, and now the boy is here too and everything stops while the boy talks to them about his dog. He tells them that Abi and he will be taking the dog for a walk every day.

No! I don't want her to be distracted. She needs to be here in the attic with me. We have to finish our book.

When the boy leaves I leave the attic with him.

'Where's Josh?' asked Abi after lunch.

'Haven't seen him,' said Patrick. 'But wherever the dog is, that's where you'll find him.'

Abi wandered down the garden, calling his name. 'C'mon, Josh, let's go.'

But there was no sign of Josh or the dog.

'I don't think he's in the house,' said Harry. 'Perhaps he's waiting outside.'

Since the arrival of Dog, everyone had been careful to keep the big wrought iron gates closed. But today they were open.

Harry called down the track. There was no answer. 'I don't like this. Josh has been told not to take Dog out on his own.'

'And why would he do it now? I promised to go for a walk with them.'

'You stay here,' said Harry. 'I'll go up to the lane.'

In half an hour he was back, the ungainly body of Dog cradled in his arms, a tearful Josh alongside.

'Josh? Harry? My God, what's happened?'

'I couldn't find Dog – and then I saw that the gates were open, so I went looking for him. I went all the way along the lane, calling him, I could hear him, making funny noises, and then – ' Josh took a huge sniff. 'He must have been knocked over by a car, but there's no car there now.'

Harry shook his head. 'No one stopped to help him.'

' I think his leg is broken.'

'Oh Josh!' said Abi. 'I'm so sorry. But you mustn't worry. Broken legs can be fixed. Don't cry.'

'So who opened the gates?' Patrick demanded. Everyone was gathered around the dog now.

'None of us,' said Brandon. 'Apart from lunch, we've been working upstairs.'

''*Somebody* opened them,' said Patrick. 'Anyone here who doesn't like dogs?'

'Of course not,' snapped Carol. 'And even if there was, no one would want to hurt the poor thing.' She turned to Josh and pulled him to her in a tight hug. 'He'll be all right, sweetheart. We'll take him to a vet right away.'

'There must be a surgery in Bridport,' said Harry. ' Somebody look it up while I get the van. Want to come, Josh?'

'I'm coming too,' said Carol.

Abi hung back after they had gone and the others had returned to work. She stared at the gates. They had been sandblasted and repaired, and new strong latches had been fitted. They couldn't have opened on their own. She tried the latch herself, several times, but each time it clunked back into place firmly and decisively. No, someone must have opened the gates deliberately. But who? Carol, Patrick and the team had all been inside the house. Besides, ever since Carol and Josh had brought Dog home from Dorchester, everyone had been careful to keep them closed.

Had there been any visitors? Postmen? Couriers? No one had mentioned it.

Walking back up the drive, she tried to dismiss her unease. Dog's accident couldn't have any connection with Marek's accident, could it? With Dog's mad terror in the attic? There was no doubt the attic floors were weak and worm-eaten, and Marek, short but stocky, with massive shoulders, was no lightweight. But none of that explained Dog's terror in the attic and his escape through closed gates. Was Helen at the root of it all? And if so, would she, Abi, have to accept some responsibility? *She* had wanted to write about Helen. *She* had found the diaries, and used them. If ghosts existed, if Helen's ghost still hung around in the attic, then it was she, Abi, who had called her up.

It couldn't be mere coincidence that Abi had changed the name of her heroine to Helen, that she'd decided to write about the 1940s and that writings hidden from view all the years since then should suddenly be made available. Writings that related the story of a real Helen who had been imprisoned in that tiny attic at the top of the house. The attic which had drawn Abi to it like a magnet.

114

There was only one explanation, the one Abi had suspected for some time. Helen still existed. Her ghost still lived on in this house. And she wanted her story told.

Slipping back into the house, Abi climbed the stairs to the attic. Closing the door behind her, she waited, watched, listened. Nothing. And yet . . .

'Helen?' she whispered. 'Helen?'

Beyond the window she could hear the crooning of ever-present pigeons on the roof and the sighing of a summer breeze in the trees. Down below she heard the insistent buzz of an electric drill, but inside the attic the silence deepened.

'Are you here?' She waited, feeling ridiculous yet increasingly angry. Was she just talking to an empty room?

'This is stupid. If you do exist – as a ghost – then show yourself. Or at least, say something, give me some sign.' She turned slowly, scanning the room again. Was that a shadow in the corner? Had it moved? No.

'OK, I guess you don't exist, but – just in case – I want you to know that if I find out you had anything to do with what happened to Marek or Dog, I'll stop writing about you.'

She waited. Still silence, but somehow the atmosphere in the attic had changed. The silence now felt angry. Cold.

'I mean it. I don't have to write your stupid book, I have

a choice. I can always go back to writing about an Edwardian servant girl, and if you cause any more 'accidents', that's what I'll do!'

Leaving the attic she gave the door a defiant slam.

Downstairs, she wandered from room to room, unable to settle. She should tell her mother and Patrick about her suspicions. No, they wouldn't believe her. No sensible person would. and her mother would seize on her confession to get the attic banned permanently. On the other hand, what if something else happened, something really bad, and Abi could have prevented it?

She should stop now, she told herself. Stop writing the book. Yet despite what she'd said in the attic, she knew she couldn't do that. She had to go on. She had to write Helen's story, she had to know how it ended.

It was another hour before Carol, Harry and Josh returned.

'How's Dog?' Abi asked.

'He's staying in overnight,' said Harry. 'His leg's in plaster.'

'We have to go back tomorrow to bring him home,' said Josh. 'He was very brave, wasn't he, Mum?'

'The bravest,' said Carol.

Josh's eyes were reddened and swollen with tears. The rest of his face was still pale with shock. Abi knelt down and put her arms round him.

'I'm so sorry! I'll help you look after him when you get him home. Promise! If I hadn't suggested taking him for a walk - '

'It wasn't your fault.'

But Abi knew it was.

She didn't go back to the attic that evening. She hung about downstairs, with Harry's help clearing the table after dinner. In the kitchen she filled a bowl with water and, as she washed and Harry dried, she glanced around the room, which was now almost completed. Oak cupboards and shelves, granite worktops, the walls above faced with opaque glass tinted a subtle blue green.

Helen wouldn't recognise it. But perhaps Helen had already seen it. Perhaps she left the attic and wandered around the house, eavesdropping on everyone's conversations. Perhaps even now she was here in the kitchen, watching, listening, willing Abi to come back and finish her story. The thought was uncomfortable, slightly oppressive.

'You've surprised your Mum tonight,' said Harry. 'Made her happy.' He smiled at her and lifted a bushy eyebrow. 'Wasn't too hard, was it?'

She shrugged.

He finished drying the last plate and hung the damp tea towel to dry. 'Remember what I said. Don't leave it too late. Families are the most important thing you'll ever have.'

'That's what Marek said. Before the accident.'

Fourteen

I didn't like the dog. He's a big ugly hairy thing and he scared me, but I hadn't meant to hurt him. I just wanted to make him run away.

How could I know that a motor car would come down the lane and hit him? There were no motor cars about when I was alive. I think they were all locked away because there was no petrol to drive them.

Come back, Abi! Please don't be angry with me. I need you.

The men had finished laying the new floors and early the next morning Abi carried her laptop up to the attic. Her desk and chair, her lamp, her notepad and pencils, all were back in place. Abi stared around the room, wondering if Helen was there.

She opened her laptop and the folder in which she'd hidden the diaries. The second diary was dated 1941, and as she carefully turned the pages she noticed that the scrawled appointments ended part way through the year, but again every page, every gap, was filled with Helen's tiny crabbed writing.

Abi turned back to the first diary and the page she had marked with a slip of paper.

I have stolen a knife from the kitchen and hidden it under my jumper, together with two more of Mummy's books. I have gradually been sneaking them all up to the attic, but there is nowhere to hide them except where the table's cloth hangs down to the floor. I plan to work on the floorboards – I noticed one or two are worn and split – and if I can get them up I can keep a few books in the space below.

I must have something to read. I think I would go mad if I had nothing but my own thoughts, my own fears, to occupy the days and nights in this tiny room. It is rare now for The Beast to let me out and it is never for company, only to clean the kitchen or wash his clothes.

He hates me. I wonder if he ever loved me. Perhaps when I was a tiny baby, or perhaps not even then. When did he find out that I was not his?

I have two favourite books for girls that my mother bought me, and I have now read both of them at least three times. One is Anne of Green Gables, and the other is The Getting of Wisdom by Henry Handel Richardson. While I am reading I am transported from my tiny prison to other worlds, where there are families, love, friends, sunshine, laughter and freedom. But then I close the page and I am immediately back in my prison.

It is winter now and my fingers are too numb to write much more. The wind whistles thin tunes through the cracks in the window, and frost flowers decorate the inside of the glass. The nights come early and are endless. It is too dark to read or write but almost impossible to sleep with just one thin blanket to wrap around myself. Sometimes I don't even try. I hunch up in my blanket, count the few stars I can see, sing the few songs I can still remember – but quietly so that I don't wake The Beast. Sometimes I have imaginary conversations with my three friends, Margaret, Janet and Patty. I wonder what they look like now? Do they ever think of me and wonder why I disappeared from their lives?

Abi closed the file and replaced Helen's notes in the folder with the others. Her eyes were misted with tears again. She didn't want to write any more. Such a horrifying story. If it were fiction, she could arrange a happy ending for Helen, but she was almost certain that Helen's life did not end in a good way. Otherwise, why would she, Abi, be writing her story?

How could she remain angry with that poor girl? How could she refuse to help her?

She closed the laptop and stood, feeling immensely tired – and cold, shivery cold, even though the August sun was turning the attic into a sauna.

'Sorry, Helen,' she whispered.   'I'll come back tomorrow.'

Downstairs she found Josh, pacing up and down in the hall, eyes darting to the clock at every few steps.

In the night Abi had been woken several times in the Hymer by her brother's tossing and turning, and this morning his face was pale and pinched, his eyes swollen. She could see he was still fighting back tears.

'What time are they letting Dog come home?' she asked

'Around five, if they've been able to fix his leg. They said it was really messed up.'

'I'm sure he'll be all right,' she said. Ghosts or no ghosts, she still felt responsible for the poor animal's injury. And then she had an idea. She went to find Harry.

'Could you drop me and Josh in Bridport after lunch? I thought we could see if the vet would let him stay with Dog until they say he's OK to come home.'

'Don't see why not, if Patrick can spare me.' Harry smiled at her. 'What will you do? Stay with him?'

'Oh, I'll probably mooch around the town until Josh calls me. It's market day again.'

Harry smiled at her. 'I'm glad to see you're making an effort, Abi. You'll feel better for it. Being at odds with your family just leaves you feeling miserable.'

She shrugged. He was right, it felt good to help Josh, and maybe she'd try to be more civil with her mother, but Patrick was not and never would be family and she was beginning to dislike him more and more.

***

At the surgery, despite the staff's efforts to make Dog comfortable, with a cushion to support the leg encased in plaster, a warm blanket and a well-worn and ragged teddy bear for company, he was a picture of canine dejection, but when he saw Josh his ears pricked up and his tail thrashed with pleasure.

'Can I stay ?' Josh pleaded. 'I can look after him and he'll get better quicker if I'm here.'

The vet smiled. 'Don't see why not.' He glanced at Abi. 'He can give a hand here if he wants. Feed some of the small animals?'

'He'd love that, but call me if he gets in your way. I'll leave my number with your receptionist.'

'Bye, Josh,' she called, but lost in communion with Dog he barely noticed her departure.

The Wednesday market was smaller than the Saturday market and there was no band to entertain but the streets were still crowded. She strolled up and down the stalls, bought herself a punnet of cherries and some chocolate, and found a secondhand book on caring for dogs to give to Josh. She was about to explore some of the side streets when she felt a tap on her shoulder.

'Hey!'

It was the dark haired boy from the group she had met on her first visit. The quiet one. She was pleased to see him. She had given her number to one of the girls, Lacey, but she had not called. Neither had any of the others.

'Craig,' he reminded her. 'Did you get home OK?'

'Not really. I got lost in the lanes outside Bridport and had to send for someone to collect me.'

'God, I'm sorry! I could have come with you if I'd known.'

'Why should you? Not your problem.'

'I was getting pretty bored anyway.'

'Aren't they your friends?'

'They're in my Year but – I've only been here two terms myself, and they've known each other forever. And my Dad teaches at the school. That doesn't help. What about you? Are you on your own?'

She explained about Josh and his dog. 'I have to go back to the vet's later.'

'Well . . .' One of the stallholders was playing an old CD of Slade. Craig stood beside her, his head turned away as he listened. She waited for him to turn back and speak to her but the wait extended to the end of the band's number and still he didn't speak. Perhaps he was just waiting for her to go away.

'Well, I'm off,' she said. 'See you sometime.'

He turned then. 'Want to grab a Coke or something?'

They sat outside one of the cafes, watching the

stallholders packing up. The crowds were beginning to thin. Again she waited for him to speak. Was he shy? Or just not a natural conversationalist?

A heavy breathing woman, laden with Waitrose bags, took a seat at the next table and lit a cigarette. Abi held a hand alongside her nose to deflect the smoke. Their own table had not yet been cleared. A stubbed out cigarette lay on a greasy plate, and crumbs and sugar scattered the plastic top. Craig picked up a crumpled napkin and brushed the crumbs on to the plate.

Abi smiled. 'You'd make someone a good wife.'

He flinched. 'My Dad says - ' He tossed the napkin on to the plate and looked away. 'Sorry – it's just - I'll go and get those Cokes. Want anything else?'

'No thanks.'

Through the open door she watched him make his way to the counter. Someone carrying a tray laden with coffee and cakes bumped into him and Craig apologised. She wondered what his Dad said. She wondered if his Dad was the cause of Craig's almost painful shyness.

When he returned she saw he'd added two flapjacks to the Cokes.

She stole glances at him. The sun, still high in the sky, created an aureole around his straight black hair. He wore it slightly long, flopping over his eyes, and he constantly ran his hands through it, flicking it back from his forehead.

The silence continued.

'So, you're not from Bridport. Where did you live before this?' she said, not really interested but somebody had to start the conversation.

'Birmingham. Dad had his own company, built it up from nothing, but it was pretty high pressure, and then he had a heart attack, so he decided to sell up and retrain. Now he's teaching Business Studies at my school.'

'Oh. And is that your interest too?'

He shook his head, the dark hair falling over his forehead again. He raked it back.

'Media studies. Films in particular. I want to do the lot. Everything from writing the scripts to shooting the film and directing. Dad thinks it's just a juvenile aspiration. An extension of little boys wanting to be train drivers.'

'Do little boys still want to be train drivers? Your Dad sounds a bit old-fashioned.'

'Yeah, he is, I guess. Anyway, whatever — I'm a disappointment to him.'

He slumped back in his chair, hands shoved into his pockets.

'I guess there are lots of parents who expect their kids to be carbon copies of themselves,' she said.

'Yeah.'

'I'm sure he'll come round. Anyway, he's had his day. It's

your turn now. Your choices.'

Craig's face lost its gloom. He was quite good looking, Abi realised, when he smiled. She smiled back.

'So you're writing scripts? I'm a writer too. I've written three books. Part way through my fourth.'

'Yeah? What about?'

'Oh – nothing spectacular. Sort of historical, I suppose. But the latest - ' No, she couldn't tell him. He would probably think she was crazy, her head full of ghosts. And even if he believed her, could she trust him to keep a secret? She barely knew him.

Still. A fellow writer – of a sort.

'Tell me about your scripts.'

A hand came out of his pocket and rummaged through his hair. She realised it was something he did when he was feeling uncomfortable. 'You wouldn't be interested.'

She smiled. Try me.'

'I film animals. And then, well, I – I sort of give them speech.'

'What? Like Disney?'

'More like David Attenborough, only with human voices. My Gran used to love some TV animal programmes with a guy called Johnny Morris, she used to talk about them when I was little. Anyway – she died last year, and – well, I found a couple of his programmes on YouTube, and thought I'd like to have a go.'

'Wow! So you go out and shoot animals – I mean, not shoot – film them, and then?'

'I add a script, about the situations they face in their daily lives. I try to make it humorous, and I try to match my voice to the character of each one . . . ' He glanced sideways at her. 'You probably think I'm crazy.'

'No, I don't. Honestly. I'd love to see one.'

He flushed. 'Oh, they're not really ready yet. Room for improvement.'

'You should read my books. Plenty of room for improvement there. I could let you read one, although you'd probably find them really boring. My Mum is my only fan.'

For a moment she felt regret. It seemed a long time since she had shared any of her writing with her mother.

She checked her watch. The surgery hadn't phoned but it was gone four o'clock. She should start walking back.

'I have to go.'

'Want to meet again?'

She hesitated, a moment too long.

'No, don't worry. I'll see you around.' He stood up in a hurry, grabbing his chair before it fell over, not looking at her.

'Sure,' she said quickly. 'Why not? I'll give you my number.' She keyed it into his phone.

Did she like him? she wondered as she strolled back to the surgery. Tim was still an ache in her heart but it was time to move on, so why shouldn't she have fun with someone new? Perhaps 'fun' and Craig didn't really go together, but still . . .

* * *

Josh was bubbling with happiness when she arrived.

'Look! Look! He can walk! I thought he'd have to lie down for weeks but he's walking!' And sure enough Dog, looking slightly bewildered by the clunking stiffness of the leg encased in plaster, was slowly circuiting the reception area.

When they arrived back at Marshbank Dog's tail wagged furiously as he accepted the hugs of all the team and a plate of liver and a huge hambone from Carol.

'He'll be all right,' said Harry. 'Although he's not going to manage those stairs for a while.'

Which will keep him out of Helen's way, thought Abi.

That evening she decided to join the men at the local pub.

'Why don't you come, Carol?' asked Harry. 'A glass of orange won't hurt you, and they've got a singer there tonight.'

'Sorry, I'm really tired, and the smells get to me now. I'll stay and look after Dog with Josh.'

'You coming, Patrick?' Harry asked.

Of course he was, thought Abi. Nothing would keep him away.

At the pub Patrick ordered drinks for the team and Abi, but then he stayed at the bar, chatting to the barmaid. The same one, Abi noticed, as the last time she had joined the team. They seemed to be on good terms. Very good terms. Patrick had pulled out his phone and the barmaid was keying something, presumably her number, into it. Should she tell her mother, Abi wondered? No, it wasn't her business, and anyway, it was up to her mother to keep track of Patrick. She should have come to the pub with the team.

Eventually Patrick joined them at one of the tables. Abi noticed how the barmaid's eyes followed him.

The singer was announced. A paunchy bearded man in his fifties, scruffy, unappealing, well-worn. He carried an equally well-worn fiddle. A folk singer, Abi decided, and lost interest. But when he began to sing, his voice was so seductive, so soft and silvery, that she found herself listening for every note. His songs were mainly Irish, slow, melancholy, full of loss and longing and regrets. She stole a glance at Patrick. He was engrossed, his mouth half open, his eyes moist, his drink untouched.

The barmaid slipped over to remove the used glasses.

Abi saw her nudge her hip against Patrick's arm. Patrick, lost in the music, took no notice.

It was later than usual when they got back to Marshbank. Josh raised a sleepy head from the makeshift bed in the dining room alongside Dog.

''I'll stay with Josh tonight,' said Harry.

'Thanks,' said Carol. 'I'm really tired.' She said goodnight to the team but ignored Patrick.

'I'll come too,' said Abi.

***

In the van Carol boiled some milk. 'Horlicks,' she said. 'Want one?'

'No, thanks. I'm full of ginger beer.'

'Did you enjoy the evening?'

'It was OK. They had a singer. Irish.'

'I suppose Patrick's already got to know all the locals. He likes to socialise. Good for business, he says.' Carol's voice was offhand.

Abi wondered if she should say how pally he was with the barmaid – but it was not her problem. Whatever her own relationship with her mother, it wouldn't be right or kind to say anything. She brushed away an unfamiliar surge of pity. It was up to Carol to deal with her own relationship problems. Maybe she had brought it on herself by taking a younger man as a lover.

Fifteen

I know Abi would save me if she could, but it is too late for that. The past is gone. No one can step back into it and soothe the terrors of a victim, change events, prevent a crime.

It's enough that I can share my story with her, that I can love her — the first love I have felt for anyone since my mother abandoned me. I am happy. Happier than at any time in my memory.

But does she love me? If so, where is she? Every day I fear that she won't come back. That she will have decided to abandon the book, to forget about me. Has she found new friends, perhaps even a special friend? I can't let that happen. I steel myself to leave the attic. I search the house, even the garden, but she is not there. She is not anywhere. Her bicycle is missing. Has she gone to meet someone? Each time she leaves I have this fear that she won't come back, that she will have decided to forget about me.

Nothing must stop her finishing my story. And afterwards, when she knows everything, she will want to stay with me forever. The days have meaning now. Yesterday, today, tomorrow. And all because of Abi.

We are so alike. Both betrayed by our mothers. Both apart from our real fathers. Both lonely. We have no friends. Except each other.

The others were still at breakfast when Abi left them, carrying a glass of orange juice and a slice of toast with her.

'Can't your damned book wait ten minutes?' snapped Patrick. 'We hardly see you.'

Anyone else and she would have apologised, but not Patrick. Anyway, what did he care if she was there or not? His comments were just for the benefit of Carol and the others and she didn't care about any of them. All that interested her now was Helen.

In the attic she took the diaries from her file, marvelling yet again at how she had discovered them. But there were so few pages left. Helen's story was coming to an end. Was it with her death? Abi feared there was no escape for the girl, else why would she still feel her presence in the attic?

She began to type.

At first he bought me new clothes when my old ones no longer fitted me, but lately he's stopped bothering. My wardrobe is now reduced to a crimson and green tartan dress which is tight around my chest and my waist, two pairs of knickers, one sock - I don't know what happened to the other - and a white hair ribbon.

I long for some new books. I've read all my old ones over and over and over again. Handled them so much that several fell to pieces.

Winter is coming again. The two blankets he gave me have worn thin and the attic is cold when the wind blows through the cracks in the window frame.

A spider lives in one corner of the window, and after every storm I watch her rebuild her web across one of the cracks.

One night there was a more violent storm than usual. It blew the web inwards, fragmenting the strands. I knew what the spider would do. Her actions never varied. Patiently, spinning in ever increasing circles, she patched a new web across the corner. I waited until she had finished and retired to an outer corner, and then I poked a finger through the new perfect web, creating a hole even larger than the one before.

'Go!' I told the spider. 'Be free! Why do you stay here?'

I knew the spider would never leave, would never attempt to find freedom outside the attic, but she could leave if she chose to. Unlike me. I should have found the courage to run away when I had the opportunity. When he was elsewhere in the house, the bathroom, his bedroom, the study where he kept his supply of whisky, but I was too timid. I imagined him following me, bellowing, furious, hitting, hurting when he caught up with me, for I was so weakened that, even drunk, he would be faster. And I had no proper clothes. And there were no other houses to run to. I made excuses to myself, but oh, how I wish I had found the courage. Now I am locked up all the time and escape is impossible.

Abi ached with pity as she typed the last words, feeling Helen's desperation and fear.

'Oh, Helen!' she whispered. 'I wish I could help.'

Could she help? she asked herself. For a moment she was tempted to confide in her mother but what could either of them do to give Helen a happy ending? Helen's imprisonment and her death, whatever form that might take, all happened so long ago. Nothing Abi or anyone else did more than seventy years in the future could alter that.

But could she bear to go on with Helen's terrible story? Yet how could she give up? She was convinced now that Helen's ghost was willing her to continue. Abi had not found the diaries by accident. She had been led to them.

She sighed and turned the page.

Yesterday morning The Beast came early, unlocked the door and stared at me in disgust. You smell, he said. Then he grabbed me, manhandled me down the stairs and into the bathroom. Get undressed, he said.

I waited for him to leave while I took off my few coverings, but he didn't, just bent to turn on the taps. When the bath was half full he picked me up and dropped me into it. The water was scarcely more than tepid. I saw him looking at me, and I had nothing to cover myself, not even a flannel.

I was embarrassed but most of all scared. I didn't like the way his eyes travelled over my body. Abruptly he left the room, returning with an old leather suitcase. I recognised it. It was one we had packed for our last holiday, just before the war started. A week in Brighton. Pebbles on the beach, ice creams, penny slot machines, a laughing clown face. Mummy holding my hand as we winced our way across the pebbles to paddle in the sea.

The Beast opened the case and flung armfuls of clothes on to the floor. You can wear these, he said.

They were my mother's. I wondered why she hadn't taken them with her.

I didn't want to stand up with him watching me. I need a towel, I said. I waited, and after a few moments he left, and came back with one that looked as if it would add more dirt than it took away. I waited again, and so did he, but I wasn't going to move while he was there, even though the water was now almost cold and I was shivering.

When I was alone in the attic I put the chair against the

door. It wasn't strong enough or heavy enough to stop him but at least it would give me some warning.

That evening as the light dwindled planes flew in from the coast again. Another raid.

Kill me, I prayed. But nothing happened and the throb of their engines quietened as they headed towards one of the big cities. I stared out of the window. If it had been larger I would have thrown myself out of it.

Abi closed the diary and put it back in her folder. She couldn't type any more today.

'I'm sorry, Helen', she whispered. 'I'll come back tomorrow, I promise'

Her throat ached and her eyes blurred with tears. She knew she would have to force herself to carry on. But not today. No more today.

'What's wrong?' asked Carol as Abi rushed past her on the stairs. 'Abi! For Heaven's sake, what is it?'

But Abi couldn't speak. When she got downstairs she grabbed a jacket, fetched her bike from the shed and fled the house.

She would phone Craig, she decided, as she pedalled furiously towards Bridport. She needed to be with someone who had no connection with either Helen's or her own life.

She called him when she reached the town. He sounded surprised but pleased.

'I'm in the High Street,' she told him. 'I'm on my bike.'

'Fine. Give me five minutes.'

'I thought you could show me a bit more of the area,' she said when they met. 'I haven't been anywhere except here and West Bay.'

'What about Lyme Regis? We could cycle there and grab a couple of baguettes for lunch?'

'Sounds good. My treat.'

'Oh no. Mine. I watched you paying out for all the gang in West Bay. They took advantage of you. Had a laugh about it afterwards.'

She stared at him. 'You were one of them.'

'I should have said something.' His face flushed. 'I was embarrassed — but I didn't laugh with them, and I wouldn't let it happen again.'

'OK, I'll let you off. You can buy me a pub lunch today to make up for it. A Lyme Regis Special, whatever that might be.'

They chose a pub with a garden opening on to the promenade and an unbroken procession of parents with children, dog owners, young couples, most of them eating ice cream, guarding it against the greedy stare of the seagulls.

Craig ordered crab salad for two.

Abi stared at her plate in horror. 'That's a whole crab! It's enormous!' She picked up a pair of mini pliers. 'What do I do with these?'

'They're to crush the claws and pick out the meat.' Craig laughed. 'But you'd better concentrate on the white meat in the centre first. Not many people can manage it all.'

It was her first taste of crab and she wasn't sure she enjoyed it, but she struggled on, washing it down with gulps of Coca Cola. The flavours mingled oddly.

'You don't like it,' said Craig, watching. 'I'm sorry, I should have asked you first.'

'No, it's lovely,' she lied. 'Just too much.'

'Leave it. It doesn't matter.'

Thankfully she laid down her knife and fork. 'Sorry.'

They walked along the Cobb and Abi recalled The French Lieutenant's Woman, a film which her mother had found on Netflix. She pictured the young Meryl Streep in her long hooded cloak, staring out over an empty sea.

'Fancy an ice cream?' Craig asked.

'My treat,' they both said together.

Craig laughed, and she felt a sudden warmth. Nice, she thought. She was glad she'd called him.

They spent another hour wandering around the busy resort before Craig glanced at his watch.

'Sorry. I have to get back soon. It's my Mum and Dad's anniversary and he's booked a posh restaurant for tonight.'

'Yes, I should go too,' said Abi, although she would have been happy to spend longer with him. She wondered if he would want to see her again.

'Er – got any plans for the rest of the week?' Craig asked. 'Like to meet up again?'

She smiled. 'Why not?'

***

In the house Brandon and Marek, armed with blowtorches, had spent the afternoon stripping off decades of old paint from the hall's pine panels. The smell permeated every room and Carol had been forced to retreat to the Hymer.

Normally she enjoyed choosing paint colours for walls and woodwork, but not today. She stared miserably at the spread out charts, wondering when, if ever, her sickness would go away. She had never felt ill when she was carrying Abi and Josh. Perhaps she'd just been lucky, or perhaps this time was so awful because she was older.

She had been so excited when she found herself pregnant - pregnant with Patrick's baby – and she had expected the same delight from him, especially when they

140

were told it would be a boy. A son. Didn't every man want one?

He had assured her that he did, yet more and more she suspected that he was just saying what she wanted to hear. And their relationship – that had changed. Several weeks had gone by since they had made love. OK, perhaps the need to be a little careful had put him off, but she was noticing his coolness at other times. Busy with the house, they spent little time together during the day but he never kept her company now in the evenings. Did he really have to go to the pub every night?

Was it because she wanted to make Marshbank their permanent base? For Patrick and the team it would mean a change in focus, perhaps lowering their sights, seeking out smaller properties closer to home, but couldn't that be equally satisfying – and profitable?

She shoved the charts aside and closed her eyes. Everything was turning sour.

***

Abi was still smiling as she cycled back to Marshbank. Nothing had happened, nothing earth shattering had been said. She had no idea if Craig would become important to her, or her to him, but at least she now had a friend.

But as she turned on to the track leading to the house her pleasure in the day left her. She slowed down at the gates and stared up at the attic. She would have to return there to type Helen's final notes. And what then?

When she entered the house she found the whole team now armed with blow torches and the stench of burning paint was overpowering. She wondered what they were going to do about eating. Her mother would definitely be sick and Abi wouldn't be surprised if others joined her. Eating outside was not an option. Heavy clouds were beginning to roll inland and the temperature was cooling. She went to find Patrick.

'I think we should all go for a pub meal tonight,' she said. 'We can't eat here.'

He hesitated. 'OK,' he said at last. 'Maybe we can try a different pub. One your Mum will like.'

'Why? What's wrong with the usual? It's got a dining room, hasn't it?' She stared at him, knowing why he didn't want to take her mother there. He didn't want her and the barmaid to meet.

'Guilty conscience?' she taunted.

'What?'

'Oh, nothing,' she said, and sauntered off. But she had let him know she was aware of his flirtation, although she doubted it would stop him.

Once again she felt a rush of sympathy for her mother. It made her feel uncomfortable and she pushed it away.

Sixteen

I tried on all my mother's clothes. The vests and knickers, the brassieres – which hung on me like empty bags because I was so thin, the dresses and cardigans. Although she was small, she had been taller than I. I put on the blue dress, the one that had been her favourite. It reached half-way down my calves. I wished I had a mirror, but then again I didn't, realising how awful I must look.

Wearing her clothes brought bitter-sweet emotions. I missed her so much. I stroked the fabrics, twirled in the dresses, snuggled into a nightgown that was made of flower-sprigged winceyette. Then came the reaction. I tore them off, hating her, hating the memory of her, hating her clothes. I wanted nothing that reminded me of her.

But later, when the sun had set and the moon rose, and a chill wind shook the window, I piled them on again, one over another, burying myself inside their warmth. Yet inside all those layers, I had never felt so alone.

Soon Abi will have finished the diaries, and what then? If only I could speak to her, tell her how my life ended. No one knows. No one.

I would willingly relive those moments if it made her care for me. Love me. Stay with me. I wish we could communicate properly, but the only way that could happen is if Abi herself died. Then we could be ghosts together. Friends. Real friends. Forever.

Otherwise I know that one day she will go away. They will all go away and I will be alone again.

Next morning Abi was even more reluctant to visit the attic. Helen's notes called her but she was filled with dread. She dawdled at breakfast, stirring her bowl of cornflakes until they turned soggy, cutting her toast into fingers and then into tiny squares, but at last she could delay no longer. She owed it to Helen to finish her story.

The attic was no longer an empty room. When Abi opened its door the air of expectancy weighed her down. Helen was here, Abi knew it, waiting, willing her to carry on.

She switched on her laptop and took the diaries from their hiding place. There were only a few more notes and as, reluctantly now, she keyed them in, it was clear that Helen's situation was becoming progressively worse. When Abi turned to the last note, she could hardly bear to read it.

He was shouting at me, as usual. And all because I'd asked him for food. Begged him for something to drink — water would do, some bread, I didn't even care if it was mouldy, no need to trouble himself to go to the shops, anything would do.

But to The Beast, that wasn't a reasonable request and he flew into a rage. I don't think he himself eats now. I think he is living on hate. And whisky. I could smell it on his breath and his face was flushed crimson.

We have both shrunk in size. The Beast's clothes hang on him, and they are stained and smell of vomit. Once he had dressed smartly, a navy pin stripe suit and a crisp white collar for the office, a blazer and knife crease flannels for leisure time, his hair always short, parted at the side and Brylcreemed, his shoes polished. Before my mother left he shaved every day with a cutthroat razor. Now his hands would be too shaky to use it. Now he didn't even wash most of the time, and his hair hung lank and greasy over his ears.

I wondered what I looked like. I could see my arms and legs, thin and white. My fingernails had grown long and I had taken to chewing them. It was something to do. I couldn't see my face but the skin felt dry and rough. My hair, though, felt greasy and knotted.

The Beast was staring at me with a mixture of dislike and disgust.

"I'm sick of the sight of you!" he said. "I've tried to look after you but you're not mine, you're not mine! I should have made her take you with her when she ran away!"

He left then, slamming the door and locking it. Would he come back? Was this the last time I would see him?

Abi closed the file and stared at the blank screen. What happened next? There were still several empty pages in the diaries, so why were there no more notes? She had to find out.

She found Carol in the Hymer, checking invoices from suppliers.

'This house is costing far more than we bargained for,' she said. 'But for once I don't care. If it's going to be our permanent home, I want it to be perfect.'

'What about Patrick?'

'What about him?'

'Are you sure he's happy to stay here? Forever?'

Carol didn't answer. Instead, she concentrated on the screen of her laptop.

'So, did you want something?' she asked after a while.

'Yes, I was wondering who owned the house in the 1940s? I mean the last people who actually lived here?'

'Someone called Aylward. Raymond Aylward, I think.'

' Did he have a family?'

'No idea. You don't get that information from the Deeds. Why d'you want to know? Is this for your book?'

'Oh, more or less.'

'Well, you can make up the characters, can't you?'

'Yes, of course. I was just curious.' Abi stood there, watching Carol make bank transfers for a while. Carol looked up.

'I know you love to write, darling, but don't you think you're overdoing it a bit? You're looking quite pale and tired. You should get out more. A little bird told me you're seeing a local boy? What's his name?'

Which little bird? Perhaps one of the team had been in the town and noticed them. 'Craig. He's not important. I've only met him twice.'

'All the same. Or you could spend more time with Josh. He'd love that. He's at a loose end until Dog is fit to play with him. Harry could drop you both somewhere and pick you up later.'

'Yeah, maybe.'

'Or you could invite the boy here.'

'To see a house that's still half-wrecked? And maybe share a frozen cottage pie with us?'

'Boys will eat anything – and he might find it interesting to see how the house is being reclaimed,' Carol said mildly.

147

She might be right, thought Abi, but she was not yet ready to introduce Craig. She was still unsure of him, how much she liked him, how much he liked her.

She thought about Tim and how much she had built into that relationship. Although she could remember him now without the sharp pain of loss, without the humiliation of knowing he had been willing to let her go so easily, she wasn't going to make the same mistake again. No, nice as Craig was, he might soon lose interest, as Tim had.

Unexpectedly tears stung her eyes. She turned away abruptly, before Carol could see them.

But at the breakfast table next morning Craig called her.

'I was telling Mum about your writing, and she said she'd love to meet you. She's written a few short stories herself. She wondered if you'd like to come to lunch. You don't have to,' he added quickly when she didn't answer.

'No, that's fine. Yes, thank her for me.''

'Want me to come to you and we can cycle back together?'

'No,' she said quickly. 'I'll meet you in the High Street again, shall I?'

'I'm going out later,' she told Carol.

'Craig?'

'His Mum's invited me for lunch.'

'That's nice. Maybe we can all get together sometime?'

'Don't jump the gun, Mother. I hardly know Craig. I may not want to see him again.'

'Still, it would be nice to meet the family.' Carol looked away and her voice dropped to a whisper. 'I miss having friends as much as you do.'

Do you? Abi wondered. It was something she'd never considered.

***

Craig's parents owned one of the houses whose lawns dropped down to the little river. Abi realised she had walked past it on her first visit to Bridport. She envied Craig, living only steps away from the busy town centre. She would swap houses with him without a qualm.

She took to his Mum ('Call me Emma') immediately. She looked like the illustrations of Mums in the children's books she used to read. Round, comfortable, complete with pinny, hair in one of those short curly styles that hairdressers reserve for the over-seventies, although Emma couldn't be more than forty five, Abi estimated.

'Any friend of Craig's is welcome here,' Emma said. 'And I hope you and I can be friends too. We writers need to stick together. Not that I can really call myself that yet. Just two short stories under my belt, but I'm working on it. We have a writers group here in Bridport, you know. You should join it.'

'Oh, I'm not really ready for that,' said Abi. Although she liked Emma, her friendship with Craig was still new and unproven. Keeping in touch via his Mum could be awkward if she – or he – decided to end it.

Craig's father appeared when lunch, a home made quiche with various salad bowls, was served. She shot glances at him, seeing no physical resemblance between him and Craig. He was a big man, although he appeared to have lost weight recently, the flesh hanging loose from his face and bare arms - the heart attack, she guessed – but she could picture him, the successful businessman, in his earlier days of health and prosperity. Well-cut suits hiding an expanding waistline, the smooth firm skin of his face clean-shaven and patted pink, the hair and fingernails close trimmed. Now there was a slight air of neglect about him. Hair straggling slightly, his blue polo shirt and cargo pants probably the first things he had grabbed from his wardrobe.

But his glance was sharp and searching before he took his seat. He nodded and smiled a greeting before helping himself to quiche and spending several minutes choosing which salads to sample.

Was he shy? Uninterested? Yet Craig had expected him to be relieved to find his son had a girlfriend. She would reserve judgement, Abi decided, but so far she was as unimpressed with him as he appeared to be with her.

'Now tell me about your writing,' said Emma when

they were all served. 'Craig tells us you've written three books already, all set in the various houses you've lived in. How original!'

'They're not very good. I've never shown them to anyone. It's just something to do while my Mum and her partner are working on the restorations.'

'Oh, I'm sure they're better than you think, my dear. I'd love to read them. And you're working on a fourth! And it's set here in Dorset! But which is your house?'

'*Marshbank!*' she repeated when Abi told her. 'But we know it, don't we, Alex?' she asked her husband. 'Perhaps I shouldn't say it, but we've wandered round the gardens and peered through the windows several times when we've been out walking. Fascinating. The haunted house, we call it, don't we, darling?'

Abi's fork halted halfway to her mouth. 'Haunted? Why do you say that?'

'Oh, not really, my dear. It's just the the fact that it's been empty as long as anyone can remember, and the look of it, so grim and dilapidated, and – Oh dear, now I've put my foot in it, haven't I?'

'No, you were right, but it's already looking quite different. And my Mum's in charge of the final touches. She's an interior designer.'

'Oh, that's nice.' Emma glanced around her dining room, in which the predominant colour was a safe beige. 'Perhaps she could give me some tips.'

151

Craig's father, Alex, surprised Abi by laying down his knife and fork, and addressing her.

'Last person to live there was during the war, I heard. Town drunk, apparently, but then, so the story goes, he just disappeared. Easily done during the War, despite the Identity Cards. Bombing. Unidentified corpses. Deserters from the army, the navy, the air force.'

'Alex!' Emma protested.

'Oh, it's alright,' said Abi, 'but I would like to know more about the family. If there were any children, for instance.'

'Oh, I might be able to help you there,' said Emma. 'I have a subscription to an ancestry website.'

Alex rolled his eyes. 'Can't keep her away from it. It's an addiction!'

After lunch had been cleared and Alex had retired to his study Emma brought out her laptop.

'See you later,' said Craig.

'We won't be long,' Emma protested.

'Yeah, yeah. Heard that before,' said Craig, but he smiled.

'I do get a bit obsessed,' confessed Emma. 'One thing leads to another, you see. Anyway, let's get started. We'll try the 1939 Census. Normally you have to wait a hundred years to access one, but the 1939 Census was a Special, carried out when war was imminent, so that the Government could know the whereabouts, occupation and so on of everyone in the country, and could issue Identity Cards'.

She clicked on the site.

'Now, what's the full name?'

'Raymond Aylward,' said Abi. 'And I think he was an accountant.'

'Hmm. Well, it's an uncommon name. That's useful.'

A few clicks later Emma had found him. 'But he's not at Marshbank. Not even in Bridport, this one is in Hampshire. Stockbridge. Raymond Aylward, aged 47, occupation accountant.'

'That must be him. He could have moved later, couldn't he? Is - is there a family?'

'A wife, Alice, aged 37.'

'That could be right. And — children?' Abi held her breath.

'No, but when the Census was made available in 2015, everyone who was under 100 years old was blanked out, on the basis that they might still be alive and should have their privacy protected. Of course, if they died before that age and their death was notified, they would still be on there.'

So the man Helen called The Beast really had kept her

hidden – and hadn't notified anyone when she died. But *how* had she died?

Emma glanced at Abi. 'Does it matter, dear? If you're writing fiction, you could give the family a dozen children!'

'I know. I just – I'd imagined there would have been – Well, Marshbank is such a big house for just one man . . . '

'Well, let's try BMD – Births, Marriages and Deaths,' Emma explained. 'What are we going to look for?'

'Births, please.'

'A name would be useful.'

'Helen – I mean – Well, that's the name of my character. It's just a guess - '

'But as good as any, I suppose.' Emma was scrolling through online registers. 'Well, blow me down! Helen it is! Born 1927, father Raymond Aylward. You must be psychic, my dear!'

'Could you – could you check the Deaths for me?'

Again Emma searched. It took longer this time. Abi tried to curb her impatience. She moved to the window. Craig was in the garden, filming birds on a large feeder. Suddenly a fox appeared through a gap in the boundary hedge. Craig swung his camera to film him. The fox, one paw raised, stared at him, and then he was gone.

'Well! That's very strange. Can't find any of them. Not the girl – no children at all with that surname – and not the parents either. Possible, of course, that the whole family was killed in a bombing raid and not identified – but no, Mr Aylward at least was still alive in 1945 at Marshbank, but whether the family were there too – well, I don't know, my dear – ah! -'

'You've found something?'

'This could be the mother, but Plymouth, not Bridport. Alice Maureen Aylward, died 15th July 1941. Your lady – that could be her. Looks as if they all moved around a bit.' She scrolled down the page. 'No other Aylwards. Perhaps the daughter was safe somewhere with her Dad.'

Safe! There was nothing safe about Helen's existence.

'Could you – would it be possible to check the Aylward's marriage? If the wife had those two Christian names?'

It took only a moment.

'Alice Maureen Aylward. Yes. So that's definitely her, isn't it? But no sign of a daughter. Still, if they moved to Bridport she might have gone to the school here. I could try the school records, if they go that far back?'

Abi had a moment of hope, but then she remembered that Helen's father had kept her at home. As if he always intended her to disappear.

Emma glanced at her watch. 'Anyway, not right now, dear. Time for a cup of tea and a cake.' She looked out of the window. 'Oh dear, here comes the rain. Never mind, we can run you home in the car. Be nice to see the house again.'

How could Abi refuse?

Seventeen

I had started to follow Abi around, feeling braver in her presence, and one day I followed her into the dining room. Others were there, eating, drinking, noisily talking above the clink of knives and forks and the clattering of plates. She sat down. There was an empty seat beside her and I sat down too. I couldn't feel the seat. I couldn't smell the food, some sort of casserole, steam rising from it, but I enjoyed being beside Abi, pretending as I watched her help herself to a portion and add salad from a bowl that I was her sister or an invited friend.

So long since I ate a meal, a proper meal. I remember eating an omelette cooked by my mother, made from dried eggs, because real fresh eggs were rationed. We had carrots and beans with it, picked from the garden at our old house. Strange, but my mind can still remember the taste of that meal.

I leaned against Abi, longing to feel her warmth, to make her aware that I was there, her friend, beside her, but suddenly my chair was moved, quite violently. I screamed but no one heard, no one reacted. It was the young man, the one with the long golden hair, tied back with a piece of string. He sat in the chair, my chair, and turned towards Abi. I squirmed out from beneath him, his weight imagined but not felt.

Abi's mine! I hissed from the doorway, still shaken but angry. Go away! But he was unaware. Smiling, chatting, stealing her attention. I hated him.

I stayed in my attic for several days afterwards.

Carol heard the door bell, a clanging sound in keeping with the age of the house, and saw Brandon running down the drive to open the gates.

'There's a car,' she said. 'Oh, it's Abi. It must be her new boyfriend's family.'

'Boyfriend?' said Patrick.

'Didn't you know? I'm so glad she's made a friend.'

'I'm afraid you're being invaded,' said the driver of the car. 'We've brought your daughter home, but actually we're being nosy! I hope you don't mind. I'm Alex, Craig's father – and this is my wife, Emma.'

Carol stepped forward and shook hands with Alex, gave Emma a kiss on the cheek.

'Delighted to meet you. And this is Craig? You'll be our first guests. Welcome!'

'We've heard all about you, and what you're doing

here. Such clever people!' Emma's eyes were everywhere. 'But what a huge place to take on. What a challenge!'

'We like challenges, don't we, Carol?' Patrick's eyes gleamed. 'Would you like the Grand Tour?'

'Really? How exciting! We can't wait to see what you're doing with it - and if you want a record of that, our Craig has his camcorder with him.'

'Never without it, are you, Craig?' said Alex, and Abi saw Craig flush.

'Even better,' said Patrick.

Of course, he was laying on the charm, Carol saw, and he was so good at that. She had fallen for it herself in the days after her divorce, when she had been feeling so bereft. It was only seeing him in action now that she realised how absent that charm had been in recent months. Since she had told him about the baby, in fact. And since she had given him her ultimatum on the house.

Abi, Carol noticed, was holding back from the others and wearing a mask of disapproval. Clearly this visit wasn't her idea.

'The hall's our current project,' said Patrick, slipping eagerly into tourist guide mode. It would be a take on Edwardian design, he told them, with cream-painted panelling and an authentic reproduction wallpaper on the upper walls. 'But it's rather messy at the moment, so let's start with the kitchen.'

'Oh, my goodness,' said Emma when he opened the door with a flourish. 'This is fabulous! You're so lucky, Mrs Stratton. And will the rest of the house be finished before you have your baby?'

Carol shot a glance at Abi, who frowned and shook her head slightly.

'I'm afraid I guessed,' said Emma, who had seen the frown. 'Speak first, think later – that's me! Sorry!'

'It's quite all right,' said Carol. 'We're actually on schedule, and we have a good hardworking team. Another six weeks or so and we can bring in the furniture and start dressing the place up. That's my department, and I really enjoy it.'

'But what a shame the house was empty for so long. Still, you'll have no trouble selling this when it's finished. Really, it's magnificent.'

'You'll get a good price,' said Alex. 'There are quite a few monied people in the area. In fact, we know a couple who might be interested, don't we, Emma?'

'But we won't be selling,' Carol said quickly. 'Now we're expecting a baby this will be our permanent home.'

Patrick nodded and smiled, but the smile did not reach his eyes.

'Oh, really?' said Emma. 'But won't it be too large for you?'

Carol laughed. 'We can always offer B&B. Or maybe we

can hire it out as a film set now and then. There are lots of possibilities.'

'Well, I'm pleased,' said Emma. 'It will be lovely to have you as near neighbours.'

Patrick smiled again but said nothing.

It was another half an hour before they reached the top floor, with Emma exclaiming as each door was opened to reveal yet another room, some fully restored, others still awaiting transformation.

'Ah,' said Alex, as Patrick led the way through the succession of attics. 'I expect you've had to do a lot of work up here?'

'Actually, we were lucky. The roof wasn't too bad, but some of the floorboards had to be replaced. One of my men went through a patch that was eaten with woodworm. But no dry rot, thank goodness.' He opened the last door. 'And this is Abi's writing room – she likes to tuck herself away from everyone and everything when she's starting a new book.'

It was a tiny space for so many visitors. Abi, hovering half in, half out of the doorway, immediately sensed Helen's agitation. Then, as two more bodies - Jake and Marek, curious to know what was going on - squeezed into the room, she felt the atmosphere becoming thick with anger.

Emma shivered, 'It's quite cold up here, isn't it? Considering how warm the rest of the house is.'

Craig, who had obediently followed the tour from room to room, nursed his camera protectively and squeezed backwards on to the landing. Josh took his hand and whispered, 'Would you like to meet my dog?' and Abi didn't see either of them again until they were all assembled in the revamped kitchen with cups of coffee and a plate of cookies.

'Well, this has been a real pleasure,' said Emma. 'And you must come to dinner one evening – I'll check dates, and perhaps Craig will have a film ready for you.'

Abi sighed. This was what she'd anticipated. The grown-ups getting all pally, while she was still not one hundred per cent sure of her feelings for Craig.

But when they were leaving and he whispered, 'See you tomorrow?' she smiled and nodded. She was not yet in danger of being hurt, and if her heart ever showed signs of becoming involved, she could always back out.

'I'll open the gates for you,' said Patrick to Craig's father. Abi noticed that the two men lagged behind Emma and Craig as they walked back to the car, and they paused for more conversation after the others got into the car. She wondered what they had in common.

At dinner that night – a casserole Carol had prepared and cooked earlier; casseroles were becoming a regular feature of their evening meals now, which Abi supposed was an improvement on packaged ready meals, but whatever meat and vegetables Carol used, there was a boring similarity to them all – the talk was about the visitors and their reaction to the house.

Patrick's face was alight with triumph. 'They loved it! Even half finished, they loved it!'

Carol stared at him. 'Good job they're not in a position to buy it then, isn't it?'

He flushed. 'I wasn't thinking – I wasn't suggesting - '

'No?'

Harry, always the peacemaker, sniffed loudly. 'Something smells good, Carol. Don't tell me we've got home made pudding as well?'

She smiled. 'Plum crumble, specially for you. I've been trying out the new Aga.'

Josh was too excited to eat. He played with the bowl in front of him but soon put down his spoon.

'Mum, can I have a camera?' he asked.

'You've got one on your phone,' said Patrick.

'Yes, but not a proper one, like Craig's. He's making a film about me and Dog, and he's putting sound to it and everything! He's going to come back and show it to me next week! And – and he said he'd teach me how to make a film!' Josh looked round the table and took a deep breath. 'He's going to be my friend! My best friend!'

Oh dear, thought Abi.

After dinner she took her cup of coffee up to the attic. She sensed Helen's presence, and it was not a happy one.

'I'm sorry,' she whispered. 'But you'll have to accept that other people will be here sometimes.'

She waited, staring out of the attic's small window. There was no view of the sea, just an empty horizon punctuated by small groups of trees, the few other houses unseen, buried in the folds of the green landscape. There was no sound except the thud of pigeons flat-footing it down the roof, off to their sleeping quarters. She wondered if in her solitude Helen had listened to their predecessors and taken comfort from the sounds of life, even if she couldn't physically connect with them.

She had intended to tell Helen what she had found out about Alice Aylward's death. But would it help? Without knowing the date that Alice had left their home, there was no evidence to indicate how long she had been in Plymouth before she died. It could have been a day, a week, months or even longer. Had she intended to return, but been killed before she could do so?

Abi thought about the 1941 diary. She'd assumed it had belonged to Helen's mother, that the brief reminders of appointments had been in Alice's handwriting. Now she needed to find out more. But what? And how?

She turned and left the attic. Outside, the garden had

the air of a stage set, the last rays of the sun striping the grass and giving a false glamour to the gnarled and lichen-encrusted fruit trees. She wandered down to the bench Harry had set up at the end.

As the sun disappeared behind the roof of Marshbank she shivered, suddenly chilled and weary. She wished she had never heard of Helen, never found the diaries, never even opened the door of the attic. Whatever happened now, whatever she might discover, what difference would it make? Nothing would change. And Helen would still be dead.

The accidents. Abi was convinced that Helen was the cause of them. Angry, jealous, possessive, what might she do next? Abi could sense that Helen was growing in strength.

It was just too much to deal with on her own. She should tell Carol, but that might create even more problems. There was no one at Marshbank that she could confide in.

Which left Craig. She toyed with the idea of confessing the whole story to him. What would be his reaction? Would he think she was weird? Fanciful? Would it put him off?

What should she do? She thought about her father, in the old days when life had been golden.

'If you have a problem, sleep on it – and who knows? In the morning you might have a solution!'

Even at ten years old she had suspected that his advice was merely a way of getting her to bed early so that he and Carol could have the telly to themselves, but who knows? It might work.

Two figures were approaching from the house. Josh with Dog, who was doing his best to hurry but was hampered by the leg that was still in plaster.

'Want to walk with us, Abi? Once round the garden three times a day. I'm getting him fit for when his plaster comes off.'

She stood up. 'Sorry, Josh, I'm going to have an early night.'

In the kitchen she found Carol, wrapping leftovers for the fridge and filling the dishwasher. Standing there alone, unaware, her shoulders drooping, she was a forlorn figure. Abi hesitated, tempted to slip away before she was seen, but Carol turned before she could escape.

'They're all at the pub,' she said. 'You should have gone with them.'

'Not tonight,' said Abi. 'What about you?'

'I still can't face it. This sickness just won't give up. I never felt this bad with you or Josh. Serve me right for having a baby at my age. When he's born, people will think I'm his grandma!'

'Patrick should stay with you.'

Carol was silent. She picked up a cloth and began to

wipe the granite worktops.

Abi glanced away from her sad face. She should say something, but their relationship was still too awkward.

'Well, I'm off to bed. See you later.'

Eighteen

I hated them. All those people, crowding into my attic. Their voices, all clamouring in my small space. I could have escaped but I would have had to pass through them. Through their bodies. I couldn't do it. I shrank into a corner and tried to shut out the noise.

Later, when they left, I followed them down the stairs. There was a boy. I saw Abi talk to him, and I felt a new emotion. Jealousy. She's mine, I wanted to tell him, but he would not be able to hear me. No one can. Not even Abi.

Is she with him now? Is she going to spend all her days with him? No! I have to find a way, more ways, to keep her here with me.

'You're quiet,' said Craig. 'Something wrong?'

'Oh – No. Just thinking about my book.'

They were sitting outside the pub that served the biggest baguettes in Bridport. She played with hers, pulling out shreds of ham and lettuce and piling them into a small hillock on her plate. If she had thought to leave the problem of Helen behind, she had been wrong. Her fear for Helen, her fear *of* Helen, consumed her, taking away her appetite.

'Look, maybe this was a bad idea,' Craig said. 'You don't have to stay, you know. If you're bored, if you'd rather be somewhere else . . . ?' He was trying to smile, but she could tell he was hurt.

'Bored? No! It's not you, Craig. Really! It's just - '

Oh God, she had to tell someone.

'Can you keep a secret? You must promise not to tell anyone – not even your Mum, even though she's been so helpful.'

He smiled. 'Definitely not my Mum. She can never keep a secret. But yes – I promise.'

Could she rely on him? They had met only a handful of times. He might think she was crazy. He might even go off and have a laugh with Lacey and her gang, make a funny story out of it to become one of them.

'You can trust me,' he said. 'I keep my promises.'

She let out her breath in a deep sigh.

'O.K. So . . . It's about the girl who used to live at Marshbank. Helen. Helen Aylward.'

The telling took a long time. The barman came out to clear their table. Craig shook his head and the barman left again. Their drinks grew warm in the afternoon sun. Pigeons and the odd seagull eyed their uneaten baguettes hungrily.

When she had finished, Abi waited. She felt drained. Exhausted.

Craig was shaking his head. 'I don't know what to say, except – there must be some other explanation. I've never believed in ghosts.'

'Neither have I, but how else can you explain it? The accidents – the diaries? I wish I could just forget it all, write a different book – but I'm scared. She wants me there in her attic all the time. To take away her loneliness. I can feel her, drawing me to her and – it scares me.'

She picked up her glass, took a sip and pulled a face at its flat warmth.

'She had such a dreadful life, Craig, and I still don't know how it ended. If I could just find out more about her mother – Helen hates her, and who wouldn't? But I have this feeling that perhaps her mother didn't mean to abandon Helen, that she planned to come back. If I could prove that, it might make all the difference, but it all happened too long ago. There can't be anyone left alive who might know the truth.'

Craig leaned towards her. 'So, if you can't sort it, you have to give up on it before it drives you crazy. Stay away from the attic. Stop writing the book. Start a new one. Those accidents you've mentioned, that's probably just what they are. Accidents. Coincidences.'

Abi shook her head. 'I wish I could believe that.' She was disappointed. Craig was different from other boys she'd known. He was serious. Thoughtful. She had expected more from him. She stared out at the passers-by, her eyes stinging with tears of disappointment.

His hand touched hers.

'Look – Abi – I'm sorry. I wish I could say something that would help, but I don't want to lie to you.'

She pulled her hand away. 'So really, what you're thinking is that I'm just a deluded hysterical female!'

'No! Obviously Helen was a real person, and she had a hell of a life. And Marshbank – well, it may be different when the work's finished, but it's a pretty creepy house, isn't it? And you're sensitive to its atmosphere, to the things that happened there. But ghosts – Hell, I just don't know what to think. But I'm here, I'll support you any way I can. Any time you want to talk - '

He was flushed, embarrassed, and she wished now she had said nothing. With an effort she pushed her fears to the back of her mind. She picked up her glass, took a sip and grimaced.

Craig stood up. 'Can I get you another?'

She nodded, glad of a few minutes alone to compose herself.

'Let's talk about something else,' she said when he returned. 'How's the filming?'

'All done. If you give me your Mum and Dad's email, I'll send the house tour to them.'

'He's not my Dad. My Dad's in New York. I never see him.'

'Oh. Sorry.'

'Patrick's my mother's partner.'

'I'm guessing you don't like him?'

She shrugged.

'Sorry. I guess we've both got family problems.'

'Oh?' She sat upright, with an effort forcing Helen from her mind. 'What are yours?'

Craig stared out into the street, his eyes following a woman with three labradoodles on leads, who was struggling to make her way against the summer tide of visitors.

'I told you. My father. He expects me to be like him. Like he was, before his heart attack. Tireless, single-minded, focussed on making money, getting one over on his rivals. Beating everyone else at golf and squash. He misses all that and he won't accept that I'm different.'

'That's sad. Can't your mother help?'

'He's got her worried now.' Craig glanced away. 'He told her he suspects I might be gay. I heard him discussing it with her.'

'And – are you?'

His face flushed crimson. 'No, I am *not* gay. Did you think - ?'

'It wouldn't matter,' she hurried to say. 'Nothing wrong with being gay. It's just – it would be handy to know, seeing we're – seeing we're seeing each other . . . '

Craig smiled. 'My Mum was relieved when I brought you home to lunch. But my Dad still isn't convinced. He seems to think you were just camouflage!'

'And am I?'

'No! Of course not. I – I like you.'

'But do you like boys more?'

'No, not like that.'

'There you go, then. Problem solved.' She thought about Alex. She had sensed a coldness there, but perhaps the heart attack had changed him. Perhaps before then he had loved his son. Like her own father loved her. *Had* loved her.

'I think your Dad's crazy. He's a teacher now. For Heaven's sake, he must see all sorts of different boys. Just because you're not like him, you don't look like him, you don't have the same interests, and you're probably a lot more sensitive – He should know better. Tell him to get over it!'

She glanced at her watch. 'I'd better go'.

Swallowing her drink down, she stood up, turned to collect her bike, turned back.

'This film . . . I don't suppose it showed anything in my little attic, did it?'

'You mean, like floating gauzy shapes? Strange lights?' Craig shook his head. 'I didn't film in there. Too many people. *Real* people. Give it up, Abi.'

But she couldn't.

They parted in the High Street.

'You'll be careful, won't you?' said Craig.

'I will.'

'Are you alright, Abi? Are *we* alright?' He placed a hand on her wrist and leaned towards her. She closed her eyes and waited, opening them again when nothing happened. He blushed and turned away.

'Must go,' he said. 'Let me know how you get on, won't you?'

She watched him walk back up the High Street, and then she called to him.

'Hey, Craig!' He turned round. 'I like you too!'

Cycling back to Marshbank, Abi considered Craig's awkward farewell. Had he intended to kiss her? Was he really so shy? Perhaps she would have to take the initiative.

But she would have to keep him away from Marshbank. She had no idea how Helen might react if she saw her with a boyfriend.

***

Carol was wondering if she could now sneak away to the van. All the building materials had been delivered or were on order, all the paints, fabrics, accessories and fittings were on hold, all the bills had been paid, and she had nothing to do. Normally she would have grabbed a hammer, a chisel or a paintbrush and taken part in whatever task was most urgent, but she couldn't do that now. Everything made her feel sick. When would it stop?

Faintly from the garden she could hear the baritone voice of Marek, singing one of his country's songs but inside the house all was silent and peaceful. She could bring a comfortable chair, some cushions and a throw into her study and and snatch an hour's sleep, but the effort was beyond her.

She gazed around the refurbished room, wishing she could feel the rush of excitement that had filled her in the past as each room was completed. The pine panelling, freshly painted, and the newly constructed floor to ceiling shelves waiting to be filled with books, the afternoon sun streaming through the huge square bay window, all these things should please her. This was to be her home, her permanent home, hers and Patrick's. Or was it? More and more Patrick was avoiding all talk of the future. Avoiding her.

The ready tears stung her eyes. This should be a time of happy anticipation. A new baby. A new house. A permanent home for Abi, who had become so distant and who, Carol had hoped, would be pleased with her mother's decision to settle down in one place. Only Josh, dear Josh, remained the same. Cheerful, affectionate, uncomplicated, enjoying each new experience – he was her treasure.

She glanced at her watch. Another hour at least before the team finished for the day. And Abi – when would she be back? There was no longer any real communication between them.

In the past Abi's writing had drawn them together. Carol had so enjoyed reading each chapter as Abi produced it, advising and encouraging her. This time Abi had shared nothing. All Carol knew was that the book was set in the 1940s. She longed to read it. Longed to help.

She had never opened Abi's laptop without permission, it was an invasion of privacy, but she'd seen how tired and stressed Abi had appeared after her sessions in the attic. As her mother, surely she had a responsibility to investigate. She checked her watch again. There was time to go up there. Take a peak. Just a peak. Then, even if she was not able to discuss it with Ali, she might be able to assist indirectly.

At least Abi hadn't changed her password. Michael, her father's first name, and 2013, the year he had left them. It saddened Carol to see it, used by Abi year after year, as if by some magic it would bring him back into their lives. No chance of that, never any chance. Abi didn't know what he had been like, and Carol would never tell her.

She found the file easily, 'GIRLINTHEATTIC', and settled down to read it. The story was absorbing – Abi had real talent as a writer, Carol thought proudly – but soon she began to feel uneasy. Did all this stem from Abi's imagination? She had to read to the end, although there was no end, just an abrupt finish halfway down a page.

She stared at the screen, the words now blurred by her tears. How could her daughter write such terrible things?

Nineteen

I stood next to Abi's mother, hating her, pleased to see her cry. How dare she read my story? This was something between Abi and myself, no one else. At first I wanted everyone to know what happened to me, but that has changed. Now it is enough, more than enough, for Abi to know, to share my unhappiness, to take away my loneliness.

I wish I had the power to send the mother away, to rid this house of all the people in it, leaving just Abi and me. Oh, if only Abi could die – if I could make that happen – we could truly be together. Would that be a sin? To make her die? What would my punishment be? What punishment could be worse than all these years alone? If there is a God he abandoned me seventy six years ago. He has forgotten my existence.

The house was silent when Abi returned home. Patrick and the team had congregated down in the orchard, accompanied by Josh, with Dog comfortably asleep in a wheelbarrow.

'What are you up to?' she asked.

'Time to start on the garden,' said Patrick. 'First thing tomorrow, get rid of these old trees, they're no good for anything. Clear the ground, replant. Too much wet paint in the house, we need everything to dry before we do any more work indoors.'

'Where's Mum?'

He looked around vaguely. 'Somewhere inside – I think she went upstairs.'

The house was silent as Abi searched. The last place she thought to look was the little attic, but it was there that she found Carol, seated at the table, Abi's laptop open, the screen lit.

'My God, what are you *doing?* How dare you? That's private!'

Carol turned, her cheeks streaked with tears.

'No wonder you didn't want me to see this, Abi. Where did it come from? It's – it's sick. It's about us, isn't it? Patrick and me! Do you hate us so much that you have to turn us into monsters and put us into this – this twisted horror story?'

'What? This isn't about you, or Patrick! It's about – 'Abi

stopped.

'I've never abandoned you! I don't deserve this hostility. I've always tried to do my best for you and Josh, yet I'm the bad guy. Not your father, not Saint Michael, oh no. And Patrick! What are you suggesting?'

'Nothing! I've told you, it's about the family who lived here during the 1940s.'

'Perhaps it is, but you've still used us as models for it.' Carol was breathing heavily and her hands slid to her abdomen in a protective gesture. 'Oh, God, I can't talk to you! But that's it, Abi. You can delete that whole disgusting file, or I'll do it for you! And this attic is out of bounds from now on. I'll get the men to board it up, if necessary. And I'm taking the laptop!'

'No!' Abi moved to stand in front of the table. She couldn't let Carol have it. What would Helen do? But, moving quickly despite her pregnancy, Carol snatched the laptop and made for the stairs.

'Stop! Wait!'

Afterwards Abi could not be sure what caused the fall. Perhaps her foot slipped on the old worn treads. Perhaps it was the twist halfway down the narrow staircase, so that she couldn't see Carol until she tumbled into her. Perhaps it was Helen.

But it was Carol who crashed down to the landing, who cushioned Abi's fall.

'Mum! Mum! Oh God!'

Carol, eyes closed, one arm twisted beneath her body, the other still embracing the laptop, lay silent and unmoving. Abi crept towards her. 'Mum!' She touched her mother's face. There was no response. Oh God, she had killed her!

'Patrick!' she screamed. '*Anyone!*'

But the men were all out in the orchard. Abi flew down the remaining stairs and ran through the garden, calling as she went.

'It's Mum! She's had a fall – '

Patrick was the first to reach her, the other men running behind him. He touched her face. 'Carol, Carol! Can you hear me? Get an ambulance, someone! And tell them she's pregnant!' He began to check her arms and legs and it was then that they saw the blood.

'Oh shit! I think she's losing the baby,' he said quietly.

'Is she dead? Is she dead?' Josh was there now, his face white, tears ready to spill down his cheeks.

'No, Josh,' said Harry. 'She's just unconscious, she'll wake up when they get her to hospital.'

'I'll call you as soon as we know anything,' Patrick told Harry. 'Brandon, you can follow the ambulance in my car. Bring Abi if she wants to come.'

'Of course I want to come!' Abi glared at him.

***

Two hours passed before Patrick phoned Harry.

'She's conscious now,' he said, 'but she dislocated her shoulder and she has a fracture to her wrist. Could have been worse.'

'Bad enough,' said Harry. 'Well, give her our best wishes. What about the baby?'

'They think he's OK but they're going to keep her in for a few days, just to make sure.'

'And Abi?'

'She's sitting with Carol. We'll stay until they kick us out. Brandon's hanging around somewhere. He'll bring us back.'

He could do with a drink. Not the unidentifiable muck that spewed out of the hospital's machines. A real drink. Whisky. A double shot. He hovered, irresolute, in the hospital corridor and it was there that Abi found him. He turned on her.

'This is your fault!' he hissed. 'What the hell were you doing? Don't tell me this was just an accident. I know what you felt about her.'

'My God!! You think I did this deliberately? I didn't know she was still there – I thought she was already downstairs. I would never hurt her. Never!'

'You hurt her all the time – you don't talk to her, you

182

spend your days and evenings up in that attic -'

'And what about you? Spending all your nights in the pub? I've seen you with that barmaid! You don't think that hurts Mum?'

Their voices had risen and a nurse paused in her hurry down the corridor. 'Be quiet! If you want to have a row, take it outside. This is a hospital!'

Patrick gave Abi one last glare. 'We're not having this conversation. I'm going to get some fresh air. I'll deal with you later.'

***

The curtains had been drawn around Carol's bed. Abi sat beside her, fingers curled around her mother's thin wrist.

'I'm so sorry, Mum,' she whispered. 'I didn't – it was an accident - '

'My fault. I shouldn't have been there. I shouldn't – I was coming back up - ' She stirred in the bed, wincing. 'The baby – Are they sure he's all right?'

'He's fine. You mustn't worry.'

Patrick came back. He bent to kiss Carol. 'How are you feeling?'

'A bit uncomfortable, but at least the baby's safe. I've been lucky.'

Patrick nodded. He stood beside the bed, shifting from

foot to foot, a hand jiggling some coins in his pocket.

'I'm going to find Brandon. No point in him hanging around. We can get a taxi later.' He turned to Abi. 'Look after her.'

He bent over and kissed Carol. 'Back in a minute, sweetheart.'

The ward was busy. The clatter of dishes, the bursts of conversation between nurses, the squeak of rubber soled shoes on the smooth floor, the sound of someone weeping; all penetrated the thin curtains around the bed.

Her mother had lapsed into a doze. Abi stared at her still face, aware for the first time of the lines of strain, the shadows beneath her eyes.

She could have died. She might still die. She had been unconscious for over an hour; what if some part of her brain was bruised, was bleeding, with no way the blood could escape?

How easily Abi had blamed her for all the changes in her life. How easily she had switched from love to hate after her father left them. How quick she had been to blame her for everything. For losing the father she adored. For losing her old home and the garden that still lived in her memory like a beautiful Helen Allingham illustration, complete with the idolised father – always laughing, always there to play games with her. The perfect parent.

Only recently was she beginning to see the flaws in the

man she had idolised. She had thought he loved her, and that it was only her mother who was keeping them apart. But that wasn't so, was it? How often had her father contacted her since the divorce? It had always been Abi herself who had made the calls, emailed, skyped, sent photographs.

A memory came back to her now. Her ninth birthday party. Her mother had invited all Abi's friends, from the neighbourhood and from school, and the house was bulging. Carol's face was flushed, she was breathless from rushing between kitchen, dining room and garden. But where was her father? He had promised Abi he would be home before she blew out her candles and cut the cake, but the afternoon came to an end, the sandwiches and jellies were eaten, the other parents arrived to take home their children with their pieces of cake and their little bags of sweets and stickers, and still he didn't come.

It was nine o'clock and she was bathed and in her pyjamas when she heard the rumble of his car. Flying down the stairs, bare-footed, she leapt into his arms as he opened the front door. He swayed as he took her weight, and his face was flushed. There was a smell of wine on his breath.

'Stinky,' she said as he kissed her.

'Sorry,' he said, and his eyes had looked beyond her to her mother. 'Difficult to get away. An appointment I couldn't get out of - you know what it's like.'

Carol had said nothing. She had never, Abi

remembered now, said a word of criticism in Abi's presence, not then, not ever since the divorce. She must have known Abi blamed her, yet she had said nothing in her own defence. How much else had Abi got wrong?

'Abi?' Carol had woken again.

'Oh Mum! I'm so sorry.'

'I've told you, it wasn't your fault, darling.'

'No, I mean – I'm sorry I've been so horrible to you. I don't know what I'd have done if you – if you'd - '

'Well, I didn't, did I? No need to play 'what-ifs?'. You're stuck with me!'

'I do love you, you know.'

'And I love you. So much. And if falling down the stairs is what it takes for us to be close again, well, it was worth it!'

'I wish – I wish we didn't have to go back to Marshbank. I don't want to put you in danger.'

'Danger? Of course I won't be in danger. The stairs – that was just a silly accident. I'll be more careful in future.'

But Abi knew it was no accident.

'Mum, there's something I need to tell you.'

But Patrick was back. He placed a large bag of grapes on the bedside locker.

'For you, sweetheart.'

How original, thought Abi.

***

Later, back at Marshbank, Abi picked at the scratch meal put together by Harry, Jake and Marek. Baked beans on toasted stale bread. Always their first choice. She cut a mouthful, but it was hard to swallow. She still felt sick as she relived the accident. But was it an accident? More and more she was convinced that it was yet another instance of Helen's powers.

This was all her fault. She should never have started the book, never chosen that small stupid attic, never read Helen's words, never got caught up in her story. Helen's ghost might be a sad young girl, a victim of terrible mistreatment, but she was dangerous. Who knew what she might plan next?

But what could she do? Who could she talk to? Harry? He would try to understand, he would try to reassure her, he would be warm and sympathetic but, like Craig, he would not believe her. No one would.

Patrick stood up. 'Anyone for the pub?' he asked.

Harry stared at him. 'Not tonight, mate. What if - ' He glanced at Abi. 'What if she needs you?'

Patrick flushed. 'I've got my phone. I can't just hang about all night. Jake? Marek? Brandon?'

Jake nodded. The others shook their heads.

'I think I'll go back to the Hymer,' said Abi.

187

'I'll come,' said Josh. His face was pale, his eyes strained and reddened. Abi smiled at him.

'You mustn't worry about Mum. She was fine when I left her. She's got some magazines to read, and - ' Abi glanced at Patrick – 'an enormous bag of grapes in case she gets hungry. You'll see her tomorrow.'

Back at the Hymer she heated a mug of cocoa for Josh, and found some biscuits to go with it.

'I'm going outside to make a call,' she told him. 'I won't be long.'

There was only one other person she could talk to. Perhaps her mother's accident would convince him that Abi wasn't imagining things.

'Craig?'

She told him how she had found Carol reading Abi's story, how they had quarrelled, how Carol had seized the laptop and demanded Abi delete the whole file.

'And then I rushed after her – and we both tumbled down the stairs. It was Helen! I know you didn't believe me, but this is proof, isn't it?'

She heard his sigh down the phone.

'Oh Abi, I'm so sorry. Do you want me to come round? I know it's late, but - '

'No. it's not safe, you mustn't come here. I just want you to believe me. Mum could have lost the baby, she

188

could have died!'

'But they're all right?'

'Yes. More or less. No thanks to Helen!'

'There is another explanation, Abi. You were both upset, angry. You were rushing, not taking care. That's when accidents happen.'

He still didn't believe her. No one would. All she wanted was someone to tell her what to do next. But there was no one.

She ended the call.

Twenty

Abi. Abi. Please, please come back. I wanted you to die, I admit it. But it all went wrong. I didn't know she was still there, and although I hate her, I would not have caused her to fall. Not with a baby inside her.

Mummy was going to have a baby once. I was six years old and was looking forward to a little brother or sister. When she told me she'd lost the baby, she cried and cried. I asked her where she lost it, couldn't we go and search for it? She laughed then, but it didn't stop her crying. And that made me cry too.

I wish I could tell you how sorry I am. Please, Abi. Please come back, I can't bear it if you desert me. Please, please, don't leave me alone.

We are alike, two unhappy, lonely souls, you know it. I just want us to be together for ever.

Patrick did not appear at breakfast the next day, and Abi heard his car racing down the drive as she made herself some toast.

'Where is he?' she asked Harry. 'Has he gone to see Mum already? Is there something wrong?'

'No, no,' said Harry. 'He's just off to sort out some supplies. I can take you to the hospital after lunch. Josh can come too.'

'Will Mum be coming home then?' asked Josh.

'Not today. Tomorrow, perhaps, but you mustn't worry. She's OK. They just need her to rest for a bit longer.'

After Josh had rushed off to play with Dog, Abi phoned the hospital. She waited with crossed fingers while the ward nurse went to check on Carol. She seemed to be away a long time but just as Abi was beginning to panic, the nurse returned.

'Your mother's had a comfortable night. The doctor's doing his rounds right now, and he says she and the baby are both doing well.'

'You'll call me, won't you?' Abi urged her. 'If there's any change?'

'Of course.'

Now the empty morning stretched before her.

191

Overnight she had made a decision. No book today. No book ever again. And when Mum got home, what then? Would Abi tell her the whole story? But would that make them safe? Or put them in greater danger?

It had rained during the night, and the sky was a sullen grey, but she couldn't stay in the house.

'Want to take Dog round the garden?' she asked Josh, and the delight in his face made her feel even more guilty.

At lunchtime Patrick was still away.

'When will he be back?' she asked Harry. 'Should we stay with Mum until he gets to the hospital?'

'Er – not sure, actually. He didn't say.' He spoke casually but his eyes didn't meet hers.

What was Patrick up to? Abi wondered. If he just needed supplies he could have sent Harry. Mum should be his priority.

The afternoon came at last, and Harry drove her and Josh to the hospital. Abi bought a large bunch of flowers on the way in. Josh pondered for ages in the hospital shop.

'Will she be able to eat chocolate, d'you think, or will it make her more sick?'

'She's not sick now, Josh, and I'm sure she'd love it,' said Harry. 'She can eat it tonight when we're all gone.'

'Where's Patrick?' asked Carol when they were allowed

into the ward.

'He's gone to chase up some supplies.' said Harry. 'I'm sure he'll be in later.'

Carol stared up at him.

'I always know when you're telling porkies, Harry. You're very bad at it. Where is he?'

Harry shifted uncomfortably. 'I don't have the address, love. I expect he'll tell you when he gets here.'

But the afternoon came to an end, and Patrick had still not arrived.

'I'll hang around,' said Abi. 'I'll grab something to eat downstairs and then come home tonight with Patrick.'

In the cafeteria she switched on her phone. There had been several calls from Craig. She deleted them and turned her phone off again.

The evening visiting hours were nearly over when Patrick arrived. He bent to kiss Carol and thrust a box of chocolates into her hands.

'Sorry, sweetheart. The traffic was terrible.'

'Where were you?'

'Those special Italian tiles you ordered. The supplier let us down, but I sourced another, quite some distance away but they were so expensive, I knew you'd want to be sure they were identical and the same quality. Took me longer than I expected.'

'Those tiles weren't urgent. We won't need them for several weeks yet. And I don't need chocolates.' She pushed the box away and it fell to the floor. 'Josh brought me some.'

She stared up at him. 'Harry was here this afternoon. He's a poor liar, not like you, Patrick – but it's time you told me the truth, isn't it?'

'D'you want me to go away? Bring you a coffee?' asked Abi. She had suspected Patrick was up to something, but she'd prefer to be somewhere else if they were going to have a quarrel – especially with the other patients' beds so close, and with the ward full of visitors.

***

'So, what did you tell her?' Abi asked on the drive back to Marshbank.

'None of your business,' said Patrick, tight-lipped, and she could get nothing more out of him, but later in the evening as she was putting dishes away in the kitchen she heard his and Harry's voices in the hall. She crept closer to the door.

'I never approved of you going in the first place,' Harry was saying.

'I don't need your approval, Harry. I don't work for you, you work for me.'

'You're going to lose everything, mate, if you're not

careful. And that includes me.'

'Shit, Harry! I just can't bear to let it go. It's the most amazing house I've ever seen!'

So that was it. Patrick had been to see another property. And judging by the time he'd been away, it must be quite some distance from Marshbank.

'You'll never persuade Carol. Not with the baby coming.'

'Babies are portable. Stick 'em in a carrycot and you can move them anywhere.'

'And Abi? The promises you and Carol made to her?'

'Abi can go and live with her father. It's what she's always wanted, and best thing for her. She hates me and she hates Carol.'

"She doesn't hate Carol. She needs her. They need each other.'

'Christ, Harry! Are you with me or against me?'

There was a long silence. Abi was about to move away when she heard Harry speak again.

'I never thought I'd say it, but if you turn your back on your family and your promises – and your one and only baby son – then I'm against you, Patrick. I won't be going anywhere with you.'

The next morning there was a call from the hospital. Carol could come home that afternoon. Patrick went to fetch her. Abi had offered to go with him but he had refused. He was dark faced and tight lipped.

'I hope you'll look more pleasant when you see her,' said Abi. 'She's going to think you don't want her home.'

He didn't reply, just glared at her. Harry caught her eye and shook his head .

'Don't worry,' he said. 'Everything will be all right.'

'Really?

'He's a man with an obsession, and it's hard for him to change. Don't worry, he'll see sense.'

But Abi was not so sure. And when Patrick arrived back at Marshbank with Carol, the tension between the two of them was visible.

Carol's smile didn't quite reach her eyes.

'I'm supposed to have a lazy couple of days,' she said. 'So you lot will have to manage without me.'

Josh flung his arms around her, his face half buried against her stomach. 'We'll look after you. Me and Abi!'

'Well, I'd love a cup of tea – and I've got a terrible yearning for bangers and mash and baked beans. The hospital lunch was something beige that slid all over the plate and tasted of cardboard!'

'Coming up,' said Harry. 'I'll be your chef tonight!'

Hours later, after all the team had taken their turn to fuss over her, and Harry had presented her with a near-perfect supper, she retired to the Hymer, accompanied by Abi and Josh.

Abi waited until Josh, eyes heavy with sleep, had been persuaded to go to bed. She was still torn between confessing her suspicions and possibly causing Carol to worry and lose sleep.

'Mum,' she said at last. 'About the book - ''

'It's all right, Abi. I realise now I over-reacted. And even if there was an element of me and Patrick in there, I can't really blame you. I just wish you'd talked to me sooner. I never realised - I thought I was doing the best thing for all of us but obviously I was wrong.' Carol lay back on her pillow and her eyes filled with tears. 'Believe me, you and Josh are the most important people in my life , and I'm so sorry - '

'Mum, the book was never about you, or Patrick, but it *was* about a real person. The girl who lived here in the 1940s. She had a terrible life, and she was - ' Abi examined her mother's face, the lines of strain more deeply etched, the eyes heavy with exhaustion. No, she couldn't tell her. Not now. She would have to deal with Helen on her own.

She put out her hand and stroked Carol's cheek. The realisation that she could have lost her was like a stab to her chest.

'I do love you,' she whispered. 'Go to sleep now.'

That night, as she lay awake in her bunk, she found herself dredging up more memories of her Dad, reliving them not as a ten-year-old but as a young woman with a greater awareness of their significance. She saw her mother's sadness, the occasions, so frequent, when her father had failed to keep promises, had been absent when he had promised to be there, had returned late at night, carrying the aromas of perfume and alcohol and spouting a variety of excuses.

Later, much later, she heard Patrick's footsteps as he crossed the yard and opened the door of the Hymer. She listened to the murmur of his and Carol's voices. Although she could not distinguish any words, there was a tension in their conversation. They were still talking when she eventually fell asleep.

Twenty-One

I am alone. She has deserted me. I have to find her, bring her back.

Always I have to steel myself to venture downstairs. The men. Big, loud, full of energy. The jolt, real or imagined, as they walk, unseeing, through me. It never becomes easier, and I feel lonelier than ever. But I have to find Abi.

The dog! Where is he? I search for him in sudden panic but he is not there. I hope he is tied up.

I trace Abi to the house on wheels in the back garden. She is there with her mother and her brother. I watch, and listen. And I see that all I have done is to bring them closer together.

When Abi awoke, Josh's bunk was empty. She could hear him and Patrick chatting to Carol, Josh's words falling over each other in his excitement.

During the night she had made a decision. She would not tell Carol about the threat from Helen. What was the point of upsetting her when there seemed to be little they could do? Abi would just have to ensure Carol didn't go near the attic again.

She dressed and joined the other two at Carol's bed.

'How are you?' she asked.

'Fine. Absolutely fine. In fact, I think I'll get up. You really don't have to worry about me. Go and get your breakfast, and I'll see you later.'

'But you will be careful, won't you? And no climbing the stairs to the attic!'

'Definitely not.'

Patrick glanced at his watch. 'I have to get started. Big clear up today, and then tomorrow we'll be tackling the gardens.'

'I'm coming too,' said Josh.

'About the book,' said Abi, when they had gone.

'No, Abi, I told you, it's all right. I was foolish – Is your laptop alright? Can you still access everything?'

Abi waved her hand. 'The laptop's fine, but I wanted to say that I'm not going to finish the book. So I shan't be

using the attic again. I'll just fetch my stuff and then —
well, it can be locked up if you like.'

'Well, that's a relief. Such a dreary, miserable room, I
couldn't understand what attracted you to it.'

Abi said nothing.

Her phone buzzed. It was Josh, his voice high with
delight.

'Craig's here! And he's brought the films — the house
film for Mum and Patrick and the film about Dog for me!
You've got to come and see it!'

Craig. Using Josh as an excuse to come to the house,
leaving her no choice but to see him.

She sighed. 'All right. Give me five minutes.'

***

Craig's expression was wary. 'I'm sorry about the other
day,' he said. 'You have to admit, it's not an easy story to
accept, but — I've brought my camera. I thought we could
go up to your attic and do some filming.'

She hesitated, 'Are you sure? Does that mean - ?'

'That I've changed my mind?' He shook his head. 'No,
but I want to help, any way I can. I want to see you. I don't
want this to come between us.'

'Well, thank you.' She found herself near tears.

'Can I come?' Josh was on his feet.

201

'No, Josh, sorry. But we can watch your film first. I hope you like it.'

The film was quite short, about twenty minutes long, focussing mainly on Dog as he manoeuvred his oversize plastered rear leg past chairs and coffee tables and through half-opened doors. Craig had given him a deep mournful voice in keeping with his appearance, an exaggerated upper crust accent, and a speech about the inadequacies of the NHS that had Abi crying with laughter and Josh almost wetting himself

'It's brilliant!' she said. 'If this is a typical example of your work, Craig, I can see an Oscar not too far ahead!'

'So, are we mates again?' He was grinning, but his eyes were anxious.

She nodded. 'Mates.'

'That's your copy of the film, Josh,' said Craig. 'You can show it to your Mum and the others. But right now, Abi and I have got some more filming to do.'

'Has anything further happened?' he asked as they climbed the stairs.

She shook her head. 'I haven't been back to the attic, but I'm still nervous.'

As she opened the attic door she tried to see it through Craig's eyes. Cramped and dark, the new floorboards serving only to emphasise the general dilapidation. The urge to choose this room could only have come from

Helen. From that first day Helen must have wanted her, and had the power to capture her.

She stood now with her back to the closed door, knowing that Helen was here. She could sense her presence – yet not her mood. Was she pleased that Abi was back? Or angry that she had invited someone else, a stranger, into her room? And if so, what might she do?

She turned to Craig. 'You will be careful, won't you? On the stairs?'

He smiled. 'I promise.' He had not yet raised his camera but just stood, as had Abi, absorbing the atmosphere, his eyes searching each corner.

He shook his head and sighed. 'How many hours have you spent up here?'

'Loads. OK, I know it's pretty depressing. You're thinking if I'd got out more, gone for walks, maybe fooled about with a camera, it wouldn't have got to me?'

'Abi, I'm not thinking anything. I'm trying to keep an open mind, that's all. You can't expect me to suddenly become a believer in spirits. Hell, I don't even go to church.'

'Neither do I.'

'Look, whatever happens, I'll support you. I – I care about you.'

'Do you?'

He turned his head away, the blush rising in his cheeks.

'I just want to help – any way I can.'

'Thank you.' Abi waited as he scanned the room once more.

'Can you see anything at all? Feel anything?'

'No. Sorry. Let's see what the camera can pick up – but don't be disappointed if there's nothing.' He roamed the tiny room, filming what seemed to be every centimetre of wall, ceiling, floor. It seemed to take forever, but Abi was pleased he was being so thorough. If there was anything to see through a lens, he would find it.

The filming finished, he perched a hip on the corner of Abi's table and smiled at her.

'Ready for the moment of truth?'

She nodded.

'If you turn on your laptop I'll send it through.'

Despite her fears, Abi couldn't suppress a hope that something would show up on the film, something that would prove Helen's existence. To Craig, to everyone. But as they watched, it became clear that Helen's ghost was not going to make an appearance.

Craig shook his head and disconnected the camera. 'Sorry, Abi.'

'Yes. Thank you, you did your best. I guess you still think I'm imagining things.'

'No - I don't know. This is so much outside my experience. Most people's experience. I don't know what to say or do.'

The film had been Abi's last hope. There was no one else now that she could talk to.

'Hey!' said Craig, seeing her near tears. He pulled her towards him. She let herself relax in his arms, feeling his warmth, his hand stroking her hair, his voice murmuring comfort into her ear. And then they were kissing. And Helen was forgotten.

Until they heard a clatter behind them. It was Craig's camera, which he had laid carefully on the table beside Abi's laptop. Now it was on the floor.

'Hell!' Craig snatched it up.

'Oh my God, is it all right?'

He took an age examining it, then sighed with relief. 'Seems OK.'

'Now do you believe me? Helen did this. She obviously didn't approve of you kissing me!'

He nursed the camera against his chest. 'If this had broken – I couldn't replace it – and I know Dad wouldn't help - '

'I'm sorry, Craig. I shouldn't have asked you – but you see now, don't you, it's her, she - '

'You have to tell your Mum.'

'So you do believe me!'

'Hell, I don't know.'

'There *are* photos of ghosts, aren't there? Standing next to living people. I've seen them.'

'Fakes, all of them. It was quite a craze, back in Victorian times. It's easy to do. But - ' She waited as he stared around the room again, his eyes hunting the corners.

'*Something* is wrong here. Whatever it is, you can't let it go on. You have to tell your Mum.'

'I can't. Not now, not while she's still stressed out.'

'Patrick, then.'

She shook her head. 'The last person I'd tell!'

'Well, OK . . . ' He was silent for several minutes. Then, 'Why don't you take a break? Come and stay at my place for a few days? I reckon Mum would be delighted, and Dad wouldn't mind – probably be pleased!'

'Shush!' She wished he hadn't said anything. Not here in the attic. Because one person would definitely mind. Helen.

'What is it?'

'I don't want to come to your place. Ever,' she said loudly.

He stared at her, his face tightening. 'All right. Forget

it.'

But even after he had left the house, Abi worried. Now she had someone else to protect. She would have to make sure he never came to Marshbank again. And now, who could help her?

She thought about Harry. Kind, sensible, sympathetic – and even if he didn't, or couldn't, believe her, he would try to protect her, and particularly Mum. Yes, she would talk to him as soon as she could get him on his own. Just Harry.

But no. Harry would feel honour bound to tell her mother, and that would upset Carol more than anything – that Abi had not chosen to come to her first.

Tell no one.

But the next day everything changed.

Twenty-Two

I was shocked when she brought the boy to my attic, angry that he should invade our private space, but my anger turned to excitement when I realised what he planned to do with his camera.

Would I appear on his film? Could I? What would I look like? I began to move round the room with him, posing, smiling, like the stars of the films my mother had taken me to see when we were still together. Ingrid Bergman, Rita Hayworth, Vivien Leigh, Lana Turner - their faces are still there in my memory. Elizabeth Taylor – I remember Mummy telling me how much I looked like her.

But when the boy finished, and he and Abi looked at the film, I was not there. I am not anywhere. I am invisible. I am nothing.

I had almost decided to let the boy stay if I had been there in his camera, like Elizabeth Taylor. Even when he kissed Abi. My Abi. But I was so disappointed.

It was easy to move the camera. Inch by inch, until it fell. But that was not enough. Now he wants to take my Abi away. No. No!

Brandon had been assigned to start clearing the orchard, now that the house renovations were nearing completion. The sun was shining, his favourite music was playing through his earphones, he had a couple of cans of lager keeping cool in the shadows, and he was enjoying working alone. The apple trees were old and disease-ridden. With his powerful chainsaw it was easy first to remove the dry branches and then to saw through the trunks. A short distance away on what was left of the lawn a bonfire eagerly awaited each barrowful of dead wood.

Soon he was ready to start digging out the stumps. Harder work, and he had managed only two when he noticed something unexpected in the heaped up soil. Heavily stained but still pale in contrast, he recognised it as a bone. Quite long, possibly from a leg. Perhaps someone had buried their pet dog here long ago when the house had different owners. He dug further, and found what he thought was part of a rib cage.

Had to be a dog, he told himself as he handled the bones, but must have been quite a big one. Uneasy, he stepped back. Had to be a dog, he repeated aloud. But what if . . . ? He pulled out his phone.

'It's probably just some animal,' he said when Patrick answered, 'but I'm just a bit worried — I thought you should take a look.' He heard an impatient sigh.

'OK, give me five minutes.'

Carefully now, Brandon dug out a few more of the bones while he waited.

'They're pretty big,' he told Patrick when he arrived.

Casually, Patrick spread them with one booted foot.

'Nothing to worry about, mate,' he said. 'Just a dog, like you said. I'll deal with them, you go and give Jake a hand with the clearing up.'

Brandon hesitated. 'I don't know, those long bones — what sort of dog — maybe a Great Dane? I can't help thinking they might be — you know? Human?' He stared down at the small heap. 'Maybe we should - '

'Oh, for Heaven's sake, Brandon! Why don't you leave the thinking to me, and get on with the jobs I'm paying you for?'

Brandon flushed. 'I still think - '

'Go, damn you!'

For a few seconds longer Brandon stood there, his face mutinous. 'We should - '

'Go!'

Brandon shrugged and turned away. But once he had

disappeared into the house Patrick began to curse.

'Shit! Bastard!' He had recognised immediately that the bones, even without the skull, were human. And that meant the police and a full investigation, and that would delay the completion of the renovation.

He thought about the couple whose telephone number Craig's father had given him. He had sent them a copy of Craig's film and they were definitely interested but he had to keep them on the boil. If he lost them, he could be stuck here forever. Once the baby was born, he knew that nothing would persuade Carol to move.

He set to work and quickly unearthed more bones. They had not been buried too deeply. Last of all, he found a skull. It was quite small. He placed his hands either side of his own head and then moved them to the soil-encrusted skull. It was smaller than his own. Perhaps a female. Perhaps a child.

He scooped the bones together. He had to get rid of them. Quickly. Grabbing a wheelbarrow and tipping out its load of branches, he threw the bones into it. The bonfire on the lawn was well alight and generating some heat. The bones were old and fragile. They shouldn't take long to disintegrate into powdery unidentifiable pieces.

With the bones in the barrow, a layer of branches on top to hide them, he headed for the bonfire.

'Stop! Stop! What are you *doing*?' It was Abi, running down the garden, followed a little more slowly by Carol.

Carol stared at the heap of bones, her face white. Her hand moved to her stomach.

'Are you alright, Mum?' asked Abi.

Carol nodded. 'Brandon told us. Patrick, you can't just burn them. We have to inform the police. There could have been a crime here.'

'There *was* a crime,' said Abi. 'I know whose bones they are. They're Helen's.'

'Who the hell is Helen?' Patrick snapped.

'She's the girl who lived in this house.'

''No one's lived here for decades.'

'That's right. Helen and the man she thought was her father were the last inhabitants.'

'Is this one of your crazy stories?'

Abi was stung. 'It's all true. Helen told me.'

Patrick turned to Carol. 'Do you believe this nonsense?'

Carol glanced between the two of them. 'I don't know. I read some of the book but I thought Abi was making it up. But if there *was* a real girl called Helen - '

'Well, whether true or not, the bones are no use to her now, so they're going on the bonfire.'

'That would be another crime,' said Carol

'Who's to know?'

'Brandon knows. He's upset. You yelled at him!'

'Oh, for Heaven's sake! How old is he? Anyway, I can deal with Brandon. He knows what's important. His job.'

Carol stared at him. 'You're turning into someone I don't know, Patrick.'

'I'm not. It's just — We have to finish the house — and the garden. Those are our priority, not some ancient bones that nobody cares about.'

'We have to tell the police.'

'If we do, this whole project is going to be put on hold. All of it. Is that what you want?'

Abi was silent as the two faced each other, her mother's eyes calm and watchful, Patrick's blazing with fury.

'Does it matter?' asked Carol. 'Most of the house is more than livable now, it's not as if we're still camping in it — and there's still over two months before the baby's born ...'

She waited, but there was no answer from Patrick.

'You still want to sell, don't you?' she said at last. 'You've no intention of settling down, have you?'

Abi turned and raced up the garden.

'Come back here!' yelled Patrick.

'I'm phoning the police! Just you try and stop me!'

Patrick started to follow. Carol caught his arm. She stared at him.

'I thought I knew you. I thought we had the perfect partnership. I was wrong, wasn't I? This is all you care about. The business. Not me – Oh yes, I've watched you. Did you ever love me, Patrick?'

His eyes shifted. 'Of course I did. I do – it's just - ' He stared at her, pleading. 'You knew what I was like, Carol. I can't change.'

She shook her head. 'No,' she said sadly. 'And what about the baby? Your son?'

She turned away when he didn't answer and slowly returned to the house.

Twenty-Three

I hadn't wanted to remember that last day in the attic. That terrible fight with The Beast.

He had grabbed hold of me, his fingers stabbing into the soft flesh of my arms, and swung me round to face him. He shook me and shook me. At last with a roar of anger and despair he threw me to the floor.

I don't know what happened next. I think I must have hit my head, lost consciousness – or perhaps the Beast hit me. But then . . . I was staring down at my body, motionless, splayed out like a starfish. And The Beast, he was standing over it, also motionless.

"Helen?" he whispered after a long frozen moment. "Helen? Say something! Helen!"

But neither of us – my body or whatever I am now – neither of us could speak.

"Wake up! Wake up!"

I waited. What would he do now?

"Oh my God!" he whispered.

He stood there for long minutes, prodding my body with his foot. But my body never moved. At last he left the attic.

I knelt beside her – it – me. I didn't know what to do.

I stayed there beside the body, my body, throughout the night. It grew dark. There were no stars, only blackness.

A long time later, when the sky had lightened to grey, he came back. He picked up my body, slung it over his shoulder and staggered out of the attic.

I hovered in the doorway. Where was he taking it? I didn't want to lose my body. Where would I be without it? The me that was left could still see, could hear, could think, could move. But what was I now? A ghost? A spirit? I didn't want to be either. I wanted to be alive. Alive.

Within the hour a police officer arrived from Bridport Police Station.

'I'm sure this isn't necessary,' said Patrick. ''It was probably a private burial, and obviously many years ago. The house has been empty for over seventy years. I hope we're not wasting your time, Constable.'

'Sergeant,' said the man. 'And we always have to investigate.' He looked around. 'Why are the bones in a wheelbarrow?'

'Just to keep them together. We didn't realise until we found the skull - '

'He was going to burn them,' Abi interrupted.

Patrick glared at her.

The policeman bent over the barrow. He pulled on a pair of plastic gloves and gently picked up the skull.

'I'll have to report this,' he said after a long scrutiny. 'There's damage to the back of the skull.'

'One of my team could have done that while he was digging,' Patrick hurried to say.

'No, this isn't recent. You may be right about the seventy years, but it looks to me as if this person didn't die naturally.' He looked around him. 'I'll call the station. Meantime, we'll have to cordon off this whole area. No more digging. I'm afraid you'll have to stop whatever you were doing while we investigate.'

'But surely – all those years ago - '

'Makes no difference. Sorry.' The policeman moved away to make a call.

Patrick glared at Abi. 'Now look what you've done! We could be held up for days! Weeks! They may want to dig up the whole bloody garden.'

Abi ignored him. She walked over to the policeman.

'I know who this is,' she told him. 'This house belonged to a man called Raymond Aylward, back in the 1940s. He had a daughter called Helen. She would have been my age, sixteen.'

'What makes you think these are her bones?'

'He killed her.'

He stared at her. 'You can't possibly know that. Not unless there were reports. Evidence.'

Abi hesitated. He would probably dismiss her as fanciful but she had to tell him.

'I'm writing her story. He kept her prisoner in one of the attics - '

'You actually know that? You've got evidence?'

'No – yes. Not exactly - ' She thought about the diaries. But how could she part with them?

'Well, thank you, Miss. We'll certainly check out your theory.'

'It's not a theory,' she called after him, but he had walked away.

Patrick turned on her. He was furious. 'Keep out of this, damn you! What does it matter if someone was murdered? It was so long ago, who cares?'

'I care. And Mum cares. And what does it matter if it

218

takes a bit longer to finish the work?'

'It matters to me. Damn you, Abi!'

For a moment she thought he was going to slap her, but then he turned and stomped up to the house.

Abi crouched down beside the pathetic heap of bones.

'Don't touch anything,' the sergeant warned.

'No, I won't.' She stared at all that remained of Helen. Femurs and ribs and vertebrae. A few threads of faded blue fabric. Tiny joints of fingers and toes. And the skull. Small and delicate. Stained, the eye sockets clogged with soil. Fragile, yet so enduring. And now exposed, to tell the end of the story.

The knowledge that these were Helen's bones brought a sadness and a tenderness. Abi wiped away tears.

'I'm sorry, Helen. So sorry,' she whispered.

She found her mother back in the Hymer. She looked pale and exhausted. Her eyes were red-rimmed.

'Mum? Are you OK?' she asked, although it was obvious Carol was upset. 'Is it – is it Patrick?'

'Nothing that can't be sorted,' she said, but Abi doubted she believed her own words.

She curled her fingers around her mother's hand. 'Mum. I'm sorry I've been so horrible. I just felt – so angry all the time. But when you fell down the stairs – I couldn't bear it if you died.'

'Darling, you mustn't keep beating yourself up about it. It was no one's fault.'

'But it was. And – and I'm scared. Something else bad might happen. Mum, I have to tell you. About Helen. About what happened to her. And about what she's been doing since we came to Marshbank. And it doesn't matter if you believe me or not, as long as you promise to take care.'

It took her an hour to explain.

'You read most of the book,' she said, 'but there's more, and most of it comes from Helen's own diaries, which I found under the old floorboards in the attic. She had such a terrible life and she's been so lonely. I can understand how she felt when I came here, another young girl. But now she's dangerous. She wants me there all the time and she's jealous of anyone else getting in the way.'

She told her mother about the accidents. Marek. Dog. Carol herself. Craig's camera. 'I know you can explain them all away, but I know it's Helen. I can feel her, there in the attic. I can tell when she's happy and when she's angry. And I don't know what she might do next.'

Her mother had been silent throughout the telling. Now she took Abi in her arms. 'Darling, I'm so sorry, I'd no idea you've been so worried.'

'You do believe me?'

Carol hesitated. 'I don't know. I'm not sure I *want* to

220

believe you, because that would be pretty scary. The accidents could all be explained away, and as for your connection with Helen, well, you've been so wrapped up in her story, it's not surprising you've come to regard her as – as a force in your life - '

'But Mum, I was writing about her *before* I found the diaries. How can you explain that?'

'I can't. But I promise I'll be careful, and I think both of us should keep away from the attic. Let's wait and see whether the police can identify the bones.'

Abi sighed. 'At least I can help there. Although there's no record of Helen living at Marshbank, Craig's mother found the Aylwards' previous address. I expect the police can trace Helen from that.'

Two crime scene officers arrived within the hour and cordoned off the site of the burial. Abi hurried down the garden to meet them. She took the diaries with her but she had made a copy of all Helen's entries for their records. She waited while they made a preliminary examination of the bones and confirmed that although not recent, they were certainly not ancient.

'Which means we now have to date them and try to make an identification,' said the senior of the two men.

'I can help you,' said Abi. 'I know whose bones they are.' She showed them the diaries. 'These are her diaries. I can't let you have them, they're so fragile, but I can let you have a copy.'

'Whatever is in them, they can't include a record of this girl's death,'said the sergeant.

'No, but all the events leading up to it are there. At least read what Helen wrote, and make your own conclusions. I may not have the actual date, but I know she died during the 1940s, and probably before the war ended. And it was here, in this house. I have the names of her mother and her father, and her date of birth, and their previous address before the move to Marshbank. Surely that gives you a starting point?'

The officers glanced at each other.

'All right, Miss, we'll take it from there. Thank you for your help.'

'And you'll let me know?'

'If and when we find evidence, you and your family will be informed.'

'Thank you.' It was the best she could hope for.

At the house she peeped into the kitchen, where her mother, Patrick, Josh and the team were now gathered. Patrick was snapping at Brandon as if it was all his fault, and at Josh who innocently asked if he could go down to the orchard and watch.

'I've never seen bones, before – not people's bones!'

'And you're not going to see them now!'

222

'You let Abi see them.'

'Nobody *lets* Abi see or do anything. *She* decides.'

Abi crept past them. It was time to talk to Helen. She crept up the stairs to the attic, crept inside and closed the door.

'Helen?' she whispered. 'Oh, Helen, I know what happened to you, and I'm so sorry. So sorry. We've found the place where you were buried. The police are here. I hope you don't mind.'

She waited. She knew there would be no answer, but she waited, and slowly the air in the room seemed to change, almost to move, and she felt it moist on her cheeks. Like tears.

***

Carol had been making lunch, a hasty meal of tinned soup and cheese sandwiches.

'Brandon, will you go down and ask the police if they'd like a cup of tea, maybe a sandwich?'

'We don't have to feed them!' snapped Patrick. He was padding around the kitchen, pulsing with fury, his face dark with it.

'They're just doing their job,' she said. 'They're not our enemies!'

She filled a kettle and set it to boil. She took a bite of a sandwich, then laid the rest down as her throat closed and

223

tears burned her eyes.

Whatever the police discovered, whatever delay there might be in finishing the work here, she knew that she and Patrick were finished.

But she would not think about that now, she told herself, as she set out mugs and poured milk from the refrigerator. And at least, whatever else happened, she had Abi back.

Twenty-Four

I had followed him. Down the stairs. Out of the house. Past the flower beds, down the path across the lawn and on to the orchard, where the trees were still quite young, with large spaces in between. They had been planted only in the last few years by the Beast's uncle before he died

He had carried my body over his shoulder like a sack of coal, and by the time he reached the orchard he was puffing and his face was bright red. He dropped my body to the ground and went to fetch a spade. I watched with horror as he chose a space between the last two trees and began to dig my grave.

No! Please, no! Not in the ground! Please, just leave my body here on the grass – let the rain fall on me, let the birds and small animals walk across me, let the sun and the moon shine down on me, but please don't send me into the darkness.

Of course, he couldn't hear me. I tried to touch him but my hands passed through his body. He was sweating with the exertion, but I felt nothing – and neither did he.

And then it was done. The soil and the clumps of grass were stamped down over my body.

And though I know that my body is no longer me, that we are separated forever, I will never forget the earth closing over my face, my hair, the blue dress that had belonged to my mother, my arms and legs, bent to fit into the small pit he had dug.

My body is gone, but whatever of me still exists – spirit? ghost? - feels even more of a prisoner. I went back to my prison, the attic. Later he came and took away the few bits of furniture, the blankets and other bits that showed someone had lived – existed – there.

Why did I return to that room, where so many bad things had happened, where I had been so unhappy? Yet where else could I go?

That night Abi slept badly, brought back to juddering consciousness by snatches of nightmares. She awoke to find her pillows and duvet on the floor, her eyes swollen with tears, and Josh regarding her reproachfully.

'You woke me up four times. You kept shouting 'No, no!'

'Sorry. You can stay in bed if you like. I'll bring your

breakfast here.'

'No, I'm going to get dressed. The police might come early and I want to watch them.'

But it was afternoon when the police returned. Apparently satisfied that there were no further graves at Marshbank, they were taking the bones away for examination but not before they had also examined the attic where allegedly Helen had been imprisoned, and had taken photographs of Helen's diaries.

Two days later the discovery was reported in the daily paper. In the meantime the garden was cordoned off and Patrick was furious.

'This is all your fault,' he told Abi.

Ignoring him, she took the report to show Carol.

'I expect they've dated the bones, and if the date ties up with the time Raymond Aylward owned Marshbank, then it more or less proves this was Helen's grave,' she said. 'They've published the names of the family and asked anyone who has knowledge of them or any descendants to get in touch.'

'Hardly likely,' said Carol. 'Don't raise your hopes, darling. It's seventy five years, give or take.'

Seventy five years. Three quarters of a century. 'I expect you're right, it's too long ago.'

So this was the end. Abi now knew how Helen's story had ended. She wondered what had happened to the

Beast, as Helen had called him. Where had he gone, and how had he died? She hoped he'd died alone and starving.

'What will happen to Helen's bones?' she asked Carol.

'I think if no one claims them, the County have to pay for a funeral. I expect there would be a cremation, not a burial.'

'Would we be able to go?'

Her mother hesitated. 'I don't think it would be like normal funerals – eulogies, hymns, flowers – and it would probably be very quick.'

'I'd like to be there,' said Abi. 'And I'd like to take flowers.'

'Well – I suppose that would be all right, but Abi, I really think you should let it go now.'

'I can't. She had such an unhappy life. I can't just forget her. At least if I go to the funeral she'll know I cared.'

Craig called her. 'I saw the notice in the paper. Why didn't you tell me?'

'I just – I wanted to, but – It felt like crowing over you, saying "See? I told you so!" And it still wouldn't prove to you that Helen's ghost is here, would it?'

She could hear his sigh over the phone.

'Even if I find it hard to believe, I want to support you,

228

Abi. I – I care about you.'

She waited.

'Can I come round?'

'I don't think it's a good idea at the moment. Patrick's absolutely furious because work's being held up. I don't think he'd welcome visitors, not even you. And - there's Helen. I think it's too risky.'

'But I want to see you. Will you come here? At least come and have lunch, Mum would be pleased to see you again.'

She hesitated. 'I do want to see you, Craig, but . . . '

She waited, listening to the hurt silence at the other end of the line.

Then, 'OK. Don't worry. Call me when you can be bothered,' he said, and ended the call.

Another week passed. A police constable had called, giving permission for Patrick to continue work in the garden, and all the trees were gone, chopped and sawn and burned to ash on the bonfire. Like a funeral pyre, thought Abi.

There had been no response to the newspaper's request for information, and Abi had given up hope that anyone remained who might have known the family.

She should at least finish the book, she told herself, but the file remained unopened. She did, though, spend a part of each day in the attic.

'To keep you company,' she whispered, knowing Helen was still there, and sensing her sadness.

***

Two days later a visitor arrived. A stranger.

'I'm sorry. I would have phoned first,' he told Carol, 'but I didn't have your name, just the name of the house. I wondered if we could talk? My name's Simon Carr. It's about Helen. Helen Aylward.'

'Are you a journalist?'

He smiled. 'No. I'm – well, you could say I'm connected to the family. To Helen.'

Abi stared at him. He looked respectable. Well dressed, older, but not old enough to have known Helen. 'Did the police send you?'

He shook his head. 'I didn't contact the police. I saw the report, but only yesterday. I've been abroad, on holiday. Fortunately my housekeeper stores all the post, including newspapers, pending my return. So this morning I jumped on a train and came straight here.' He beckoned down the drive. 'I have a taxi waiting outside. May I send it away?'

Patrick, Harry and Jake were upstairs, and Brandon and Marek were pressure washing the old external brickwork. All were within call. And the man did look harmless.

She nodded.

'Thank you.'

They watched him walk back down the drive.

'Do you think he's genuine?' asked Abi.

'We'll see,' said Carol.

On his return they took him into the drawing room, which had now been fully decorated and made comfortable with some of the furniture they had taken out of storage.

'Do sit down,' said Carol. 'Would you like coffee?'

'Thank you.'

Carol nodded to Abi, who reluctantly headed to the kitchen, returning in record time with a tray of drinks and some biscuits.

'Well, Mr Carr,' said Carol. 'What's this connection you mention?'

He took a sip of his coffee and replaced the cup on the tray. 'I think – I *hope* – Helen Aylward is my sister.'

Carol put her own cup down. 'How old are you, Mr Carr?'

'Sixty nine.'

'Then you can't possibly have known her. She died over seventy five years ago.'

'You're right, I didn't know her. But we had the same father. His name was David Carr.' He looked at them both as if expecting them to recognise the name.

'There *was* another man, and Helen was his child. But she didn't know his name,' said Abi. She stared at the man. She had a picture of Helen in her head, small, dark haired, slight of build. But this man sitting before her was heavily built and his hair, although thinning, was a light brown, thatched with white.

'I'll tell you everything I know, and you can decide whether it's the truth or not,' he said.

***

Patrick was in a foul mood. The couple who were interested in Marshbank had called him twice since the notice had appeared in the paper. They were still interested, they said – in fact it was all quite exciting – but they now had a firm buyer for their own property and really needed to move quite quickly, so when did he think the renovation would be completed, and would the discovery cause any more delay?

He measured another length of wisteria-patterned wallpaper and began to paste it. The choice of paper had been Carol's, as had the room, the largest bedroom which faced the sea and which also had a small ante room, perfect, she said, for a nursery.

Damn the police! Damn Abi! Damn this Helen who, if she'd ever existed, was still causing havoc. He didn't

232

believe in ghosts – how could any sensible person? – but Abi did, and she was determined to obstruct him. As for Carol, and the baby . . . He stopped short of examining his real feelings there.

Was he the only one amongst them who gave even a passing thought to what was their livelihood? The source of income for him and the family? The source that paid the wages to Harry and Jake and Marek and Brandon?

Harry tried to calm him.

'Be patient, Patrick. It's only been a few weeks, and there's still plenty of work in the house to keep the men occupied. You have to forget the place in Norfolk, you know Carol won't move again. Stop dreaming, mate. None of us are going to starve, bound to be plenty of work in this area to keep us all going.'

'Rich people wanting an extension for a party room or an indoor pool?' Patrick jeered. 'Kitchens and bathrooms? I'm not going to step backwards, Harry. I'm good at what I do. *We're* good at what we do. This is my life and no so-called ghost is going to ruin it.'

'And no baby either?' asked Harry gently.

'Damn you, Harry!' Patrick flung down the cloth he had been using to smooth the paper and stalked from the room, kicking over the bucket of paste as he went.

Harry sighed and began to scrape the paste off the freshly varnished floorboards.

'My mother died thirty five years ago,' said Simon Carr. 'I think she and my father had a reasonably happy marriage, although with hindsight I realise that something was missing. It wasn't until after her burial that he told me about Helen. And her mother, Alice Aylward.'

Abi gripped her mother's hand. 'He knew them?'

Simon nodded. 'Helen was his daughter.'

So David Carr was Alice's 'fancy man', as Raymond Aylward had described him.

'When he and Alice were very young, still in their teens, they were sweethearts. But then the inevitable happened – Alice got pregnant. Her parents sent her away to have the baby. She was supposed to give it up for adoption but she refused, and brought Helen home with her.

'Meanwhile my father was away at sea. He was a naval recruit, and it was his first major voyage. He was away for months. Alice hadn't written, perhaps she wanted to tell him in person, so he knew nothing about the birth. When he returned he wanted to marry Alice, but although it would have made her 'respectable', her parents refused. They had someone else in mind, an older man, an accountant with his own business, his own house, and a safe income.'

Simon paused, and took a sip of his coffee, now barely warm. 'Nowadays she would have made her own choice,

234

but then – she was still under age and under her parents' control.'

'So she married Raymond Aylward.' Abi glanced at her mother. 'And he took on the baby. Helen.'

Simon nodded. 'But my father kept in touch. In between voyages, he and Alice arranged to meet. She would bring Helen with her. Sometimes it would be an afternoon, even a whole day, other times just an hour. Although Alice's husband suspected, he could never prove anything.'

'But he did suspect,' said Abi. 'And he took it out on Alice – and later on Helen herself.'

'Yes, sadly. Anyway, this went on for years – my father never stopped loving Alice, although he wasn't able to see Helen again once she learned to talk. They were both worried that the child might give them away. He tried to persuade Alice to leave her husband, but my father's own career meant she and Helen would have spent most of their time alone.

'And then came the War. They still managed to get together, mostly in Plymouth, but only when my father was on leave.'

Carol interrupted. 'Did he tell you all this, Simon? What about your mother? Did she know?'

'They didn't meet until after the War. They married in 1946 and I was born in 1950.' Simon hesitated. 'He did genuinely care for her and I think she was quite content.

But Alice was the big love of his life, and when she died - '

'When she *died?'* said Abi. 'He knew?'

Simon nodded. 'She was caught in the last big blitz on Plymouth. 1941. My father didn't find out until two weeks later when he discovered her name on a list of bodies identified. He was devastated. He felt guilty ever after. If she hadn't been to see him she would have been safe.

'But there was still Helen. His daughter. And he wanted to make her his responsibility. So he went to visit Raymond Aylward, only to find that he and Helen had disappeared. No one knew where. And it was wartime. People disappeared all the time. Soldiers were killed in battle. Others deserted. People were bombed and it wasn't always possible to identify their remains. People stole away during the blackouts. Criminals found it easy to lie low. My father had no identification, just their names, and he didn't know where to start.'

Abi leaned forward. 'Where were they living when Alice was still alive?'

'In Hampshire. A small town called Stockbridge.'

She nodded and glanced at her mother. 'That's right.'

'I remember my father disappearing from time to time. Said he was going climbing, which my mother was never interested in doing. It was only after my mother died that he told me where he had been on those trips. Searching town after town, looking in old newspapers, checking documents. But he never found anything.'

236

'How sad,' said Carol. 'He must have loved them both so much.'

'Yes.'

Simon was quiet for a long time but then he seemed to shake himself. 'My father paid for Alice's funeral and her grave. Raymond Aylward couldn't be found at his last address and he never came forward, so my father pretended to be him - no one queried it - and he had her buried in Plymouth. The gravestone just had her first name on it, no surname. "Alice. Born 1909. Died 1941. Forever loved." And when my father was dying, he asked that he be buried, not with Sylvia, his wife, but alongside Alice. So. There he lies.'

The door opened. It was Patrick. 'The men are getting hungry, Carol. D'you want me to book a meal at the pub?' He saw Simon. 'Oh. Sorry, I didn't know we had a visitor.'

'This is Simon Carr, Patrick,' said Carol. 'He's a relative of Helen's'

'Oh! Well, that's great. Does that mean we'll be able to get on with our work here?'

'Patrick!' Carol turned to Simon. 'I'm sorry, Mr Carr. My partner's very concerned about our business at the moment.'

Simon rose from his seat. 'That's all right. I've kept you long enough.'

'Unless you'd like to join us at the local pub?' said Abi,

237

unwilling to let him go.

'No, thank you, I'm booked in overnight at a pub in Bridport.' He hesitated. 'I'll be talking to the local police in the morning. Then – may I come back and talk to you some more?'

'You must,' said Abi. 'Please don't go without telling us the rest of the story!'

Twenty-Five

For so long I have tried not to think about my death, and now that is impossible. It is all around me. From my window I watched the policemen and other men in white overalls working over the ground where I was buried, and examining other parts of the garden.

I can feel the pull, an almost overpowering curiosity, to go down there and look at my burial place. My bones are gone. Would I have liked to see them? I don't know how that would make me feel. Already the discovery is upsetting me. The only thing that pleases me is that Abi knows everything and is spending time with me every day.

She loves me. I know that now. And as long as she is here, as long as she returns to my attic, I tell myself I will be content.

The next day as the hours passed Abi feared Patrick had driven Simon away.

'Or maybe he's just an attention seeker,' Patrick said, when she tackled him. 'Some sort of ghoul.'

'I don't believe that,' said Carol, 'and if you'd been there to hear him from the beginning, neither would you.'

'Then why hasn't he come back?'

It was late afternoon when Simon did return.

'I'm sorry. I've been with the police most of the day. Not sure if they believed me, but they're now checking my DNA against Helen's for matches.' He smiled. 'They were also checking me out as a possible murderer until I told them I wasn't born until five years after the War ended!'

'So what happens now?' asked Carol.

He shrugged. 'I don't think they've got any leads. I told them Helen's mother was an only child, so it's unlikely they'll turn up any other relatives, and they'd already checked through Aylward's family. I expect Helen will just become another Cold Case and be filed away.

'So . . . ' He leaned forward, his eyes focussing on Carol, Abi and finally Patrick, who had insisted on being present. 'I've asked if I could have Helen's bones when they've closed the investigation.'

Patrick sat up, 'What do you want them for?' He turned to Carol and Abi. 'How do we know he's telling the truth?'

'Can we not squabble over who keeps them, Patrick!' snapped Carol. 'Anyway, surely it's in your interests for someone else to deal with them, and then you can get on with whatever you're planning for this house!'

'All right. All right!' Patrick checked his watch. 'I've got work to do.' He nodded to Simon and stomped out of the room, slamming the door behind him.

'I must apologise for my partner,' said Carol. 'He's very stressed at the moment.'

'No need,' said Simon. 'I understand. All this – it must have been a shock.'

Carol stood up. 'Can I get you anything, Simon? I'm just going to make drinks for our team.'

'No, thanks, I need to collect my things and catch a train home. But thank you for listening. I'll get in touch when I hear more from the police.'

'Before you leave,' said Abi , after Carol had gone, 'I wondered – I don't suppose you have any photographs of Helen?'

'Actually, I do. After Alice had to leave Helen at home, she used to bring photographs to my father whenever they met. Here, I have a couple in my wallet.'

So I was right, thought Abi as she examined the two black and white photographs he pulled out. There was Helen, twelve or thirteen, smiling for the camera. She was as Abi had pictured her, slight of build, a thin face, dark hair held back with an Alice band. The other photograph showed her as a toddler dressed in a frilly dress and clutching a kitten to her chest. In both photographs she looked happy and carefree.

She gave them back reluctantly.

'Do you have a family, Simon?' she asked.

'I'm divorced but I have a son and a daughter and three grandchildren.' He was silent for a moment, and then - 'If the police allow me to take Helen, then there'll be a funeral, just something private. If you'd like to come - ?'

'I'd love to.' Abi hesitated. 'Simon, would you come up to Helen's attic with me?'

He glanced at his watch. 'All right, but I don't have long. My train - '

'We won't be long.'

She led the way up the two flights of stairs, hoping they wouldn't meet Patrick on the way.

'This is where he kept her prisoner,' she said. 'I think he might even have killed her in this attic.'

She turned to Simon. 'Do you believe in ghosts? Because Helen's ghost is still here. She never left.'

Simon stared around the tiny cramped room.

'She showed me where to find the diaries she kept.' Abi moved her foot across the floor. 'Here, under the original floorboards. I've printed copies for you, and a copy of my story too. When you've read them, I think – I hope - you'll believe.'

She laid her hand on his sleeve. 'You won't see her. Or hear her. But she's here. She communicates with me, gets inside my head. Could you – would you say something to her?'

'Oh – I really - '

' *Please* - '

He flushed, self-conscious. 'What should I say?'

'Just tell her who you are – and what you're going to do. *Please*?'

Hesitant at first, he began to speak.

'Er – my name is Simon Carr. I've known about – about you - for years. Helen. I carried on the search for you after my father, *our* father, died. And now we - I've found you.' He cleared his throat. 'Our father – your real father - and your mother are buried together in a cemetery in Plymouth. Now, if I'm allowed, I want to take your – your remains and bury them in the same grave, so that you'll all be together, at last.'

He turned to Abi. 'Is that all right?'

'Wonderful. Thank you.'

After he had gone, Abi returned to the attic.

'See, Helen? You're not alone any more. You have a half brother. His father, David, was your father – your real

243

father. And David spent half his life searching for you after your mother was killed. Yes, killed. She never left you. She meant to come back to you but she died in the Blitz in Plymouth. You had a mother and a father, Helen. And they both loved you.'

***

Afterwards, sitting in the train, unable to concentrate on the newspaper he had grabbed at the station, Simon wondered what he had experienced. He didn't believe in ghosts, of course he didn't. The whole thing had been an embarrassment, and he had seen nothing, heard nothing. Yet afterwards his head, his heart, had been flooded by a wave of joy that came from somewhere outside his body.

***

At breakfast a few days later Carol received a call from Craig's mother.

'You must be having such a difficult time,' she said. 'I wondered if you'd like to come for lunch? Such a shock! I can't imagine how you must be feeling. Do come, I'm sure you need a break. Bring Abi and Josh. And Patrick, if he's not too busy.'

Patrick, as Carol expected, refused. 'I don't have time. And what can they do for us? Nothing.'

'They just want to be friends. You know what friends are, Patrick?' But he was already out of the door, snapping at Brandon who was putting a final polish on the hall's oak flooring.

Josh was delighted. He rushed to find his sister.

'We're going to my friend Craig's house, Abi! For lunch! You're invited too! I'm going to ask if Dog can come!'

Abi sighed. She wondered if this was Craig's doing. There had been no contact since the discovery of Helen's bones. Even now, even after the camera incident, she wasn't sure he was convinced that Helen still existed and that there was danger in arousing her anger.

On the journey there Josh, with his beloved companion panting on the seat beside him and filling the car with pungent essence of dog, filled them in on the day's agenda.

'We're all going to have lunch and then me and Craig are going to take Dog for a walk – they live by the river, Mum! You can come too, Abi. And Craig says his Dad liked the film – my Dog film! – and he's going to contact someone he knows in a film production company!'

Ah! So that relationship was improving.

***

Emma and Alex met them at their front door.

'Welcome!' said Emma, arms outstretched to embrace them all. 'And this is our movie star!' She bent to pat Dog.

'D'you think he should have a haircut?' asked Josh. 'And I was wondering if I should give him a surname? You know, there may be other dogs called Dog, and if he's going to be famous we don't want them to be mixed up.'

245

'That's not likely to happen, Josh,' said Emma. 'There can't be any others like this one, I'm sure.'

Carol turned to the river.

'You have such a lovely situation here. So quiet. You'd never know the town was just a few metres away.'

'Yes, we've been here years, but we still love it. Come in, come in.'

'Craig?' she called up the stairs. 'They're here. He's up in his room, editing yet another film. Craig! They're here.'

She led them straight into the dining room, where the table was laid for a full three course meal.

'I may have gone slightly over the top,' she said anxiously, 'but I don't suppose you have time to spend in the kitchen now, Carol – all those police officers and reporters – did you see the article in the paper? - while you're rushing to finish the house!'

'Oh, there's no rush,' said Carol. Her hand moved to her stomach. 'As long as it's finished before the baby comes.'

'Oh, but –' Emma glanced at Alex. 'I thought – '

'Our friends, Adam and Charlotte, their own purchaser wants to be in next month,' said Alex. 'Patrick said – '

'Yes? What did Patrick say?'

'No, we must have got it wrong.' Emma laid her hand on Alex's arm. 'Silly of us, we just assumed you'd come to an agreement. Wrong end of the stick. Not your house. Some other house. Not yours. Now then. Lunch. We have a wonderful butcher in Bridport, I got some lovely venison steaks. Low calorie, you know. Easy on the hips,' Emma babbled, as she ushered them to their seats. 'Craig! Ah, there you are. Do sit down, everyone, mustn't let it get cold.'

Craig nodded and smiled, but there was a question in his eyes as his gaze met Abi. She hesitated, then smiled back.

'So I gather the police have confirmed the bones belong to this young girl, Helen Aylward?' said Alex, when the soup and the main course had been cleared away and Emma had produced a steaming blackcurrant and apple sponge for dessert.

'Wow!' said Josh his eyes huge with delight.

Carol smiled. 'I do feed him, you know.' She turned to Alex. 'A relative turned up – a half brother, born much later. The police checked his DNA against Helen's and they've confirmed the relationship. So now he wants to re-bury the bones with her mother and her real father.'

Alex raised his eyebrows. 'And is that likely to happen?'

'Yes,' said Abi. 'It has to! I want Helen to have a proper funeral at last – and I want to be there.'

'So this Raymond Aylward – who might have been her murderer - wasn't her real father?'

'Definitely not,' said Abi. 'And no one knows what happened to him. He just disappeared.'

'Well!' Alex leaned back in his chair. 'I understand you've been very involved in this, Abi.'

'Yes.'

'Putting it all in a book? Shouldn't have any trouble finding a publisher. I have a contact, might be interested?'

Abi thought about it. If it was successful hundreds, perhaps thousands, of people would know what happened to Helen.

'I'm not sure that's what Helen wants.'

In the silence that followed, Craig stood up.

'Ready for that walk, Josh?'

'Yes!' Josh had left Dog in the hall, and mournful reminders were filtering through to the dining room that he'd been ignored long enough.

'Abi? Want to come?'

***

'So, are things better with your Dad?' she asked while Josh was searching for a stick to throw.

'It couldn't go on. Mum was unhappy, Dad was - ' Craig shrugged. 'I suggested we sit down and talk it out. Dad was still worrying that I might be gay and that upset Mum. It wouldn't have bothered her, she's OK with it, but Dad, he's old school and – he was always pretty macho before he had his heart attack, and he wanted me to be the same.

'Anyway, we talked it through, and afterwards he watched a couple of my films and had a laugh at them. It helped, too, that I'd been seeing you. That was the clincher.'

'So is that why you kept phoning me?' Abi teased. 'To provide evidence?'

Craig turned to her. 'No, I was worried, and I wanted to see you. Protect you if necessary.'

'From what?'

'From whatever. Your own fears, I suppose.'

They walked on. Josh and Dog were ahead of them, with Josh struggling to keep Dog out of the river.

'You know, it would have been so much easier to pretend I believed you,' said Craig. 'I'd support you in anything but I don't want there to be any lies between us, ever. In fact - '

He was silent for a moment. 'I really like you, Abi. *Really* like you – but I don't expect you to feel the same way. You mustn't think - '

She put a finger to his lips. 'It's OK. I like you too. I just didn't want you to get hurt. But I think Helen's happy now.' She told him about Simon's visit. 'He's got permission to take her remains back to Plymouth and have them buried with those of her mother and her real father. There's going to be a proper funeral service, and that should be the end of it.'

They had arrived back at Craig's home. He paused at the gate.

'I'd like to come,' he said. 'To the funeral. If you don't mind?'

She nodded, and felt a sudden desire to weep. 'Thank you.'

***

Afterwards, as the family were leaving, Emma caught Carol's arm.

'I'm so sorry about the mix-up. The house. I always get things wrong!'

Carol smiled sadly. 'You didn't this time.'

Twenty-Six

I have a brother.

I wish I could cry. I can still remember how it felt, to let the tears fall, to sob, to make noises, to release all the hard, burning, hateful thoughts and the ice-cold fluttery fears that filled my life in those last few years. I want to cry now, I want to feel again the joy I felt when he came to my attic.

Simon Carr. An old man with grey hair and kind eyes. My brother. And I had a father, a real father. Abi told me how both of them spent years searching for me.

It should be enough. To know that my real father cared about me. Loved me. Tried all his life to find me.

But it isn't. I need <u>her</u>. My mother. At first, when they said she did not abandon me, that she intended to come back home but lost her life to a bomb, I was so happy. But *seventy six years have passed since she left me. Three quarters of a century. In all those passing years, why has she not found me again?*

Where is she? Did she not search for me? If I was a mother and had been separated from my child I would have searched forever. I would have searched every house in the country, in the world. I would have flown across the land and the oceans, searching day and night. I would never have given up.

A real mother, a loving mother, would have done that, wouldn't she? I was just fourteen, and very frightened.

If she had searched for me, if she is still searching for me, if by any chance her spirit is there at the grave of my father and herself, then she has only to follow Abi home to find me.

She must come to me. Only then will I believe that she truly cares for me. Only then can I forgive her.

And now I am going to lose Abi. She and her mother are reconciled and I am lonelier than ever.

But even if I could still cry, there will be no tears now. I feel nothing.

Do what you like with my bones. They are not me.

I am me. Here in this attic.

Twenty-Seven

Stripped of furniture and personal possessions, the rooms at Marshbank echoed to Abi's footsteps. Patrick and her mother with elaborate politeness had divided everything between them. Mine. Yours. Mine. Yours.

Everything except the baby. Although Patrick had promised to return regularly once his son was born, Abi suspected his visits wouldn't be too frequent.

It had all happened so quickly, but Patrick was gone now. Harry and the team gone, too. Abi would miss them. Harry and Brandon had promised to keep in touch, but people always said that, didn't they? But maybe Harry would keep his promise. Josh had clung to him until Patrick had to force his arms apart.

The Hymer was gone, with no regrets from Carol or Abi, or even Josh, who was thrilled with the prospect of living just a few streets away from his hero, Craig. Carol had bought a small nineteenth century house with an empty shop attached, and after the baby was born she planned to sell imported French furniture, fabrics, and accessories. Emma was to be her first customer. 'Time to get rid of all that beige!' she had joked.

Meanwhile Abi and Josh were enrolled in Bridport schools, Josh for his final year at primary school, Abi at senior school, in the same year as Craig. She had renewed her acquaintance with the cycling group she had met earlier in the summer, but was in no hurry to befriend them. It was enough that she had Craig, that she had the prospect of a settled future, that she and her mother were friends again. And that Helen was at peace and no longer a danger.

She climbed the stairs to the attic for the last time. She could no longer sense Helen's presence. Her bones now lay beneath the earth in the Plymouth cemetery, close to those of her mother and father. Her spirit? Was there a Heaven? Abi hoped that Helen was up there now, reunited forever with her mother, meeting at last the father she had never known.

Helen's funeral had been a quiet, private service in the church that Simon Carr himself attended, with just Simon's own family, Abi, her mother and Craig in the front pews. The church was small and unassuming. There were no flowers, no elaborate decoration, but a sense of peace emanated from the old stones. Afterwards there had been the interment within the grave of Helen's parents. The sun, which had been hiding behind a thin blanket of cloud, came out briefly as if to give its blessing. Both ceremonies had been simple but moving, and Abi had found herself fighting back tears.

'My father would have been so pleased,' said Simon.

'Do you think he knows? Do you think all three of them, their souls, are together now?'

He hesitated. 'I would very much like to think so.'

'Me too.' But Abi still doubted. She had hoped Helen would be there, at the church, at the grave. She had imagined her hitching a ride in the car to Plymouth, following them into the church, listening to the service, following them to the cemetery for a joyous reunion. Abi had expected to feel her presence but there had been nothing. What if Helen had been too frightened to leave her attic, like an animal kept in captivity for decades, unable to leave its cage when the gate was opened?

And how would Helen's parents know that the remains of their daughter were now snugly buried with their own? It might be comforting for those still alive to bury their loved ones together, but could you ever be sure the loved ones had got the message?

How *did* souls meet after death? If the spirits of Helen and her mother hadn't been able to find each other in three quarters of a century, why would it be any easier now, in a world without boundaries, amongst the multitudes of the dead stretching back over millennia? But perhaps the Golden Gates of Heaven really did exist.

Perhaps St Peter was there, clipboard at the ready, able to match up the newly dead with the long dead, or the newly buried with the long buried. Perhaps all stories eventually had a happy ending. Abi hoped so.

Back home at Marshbank Abi had been tempted to continue with Helen's story and take up Alex's offer of an introduction to his publisher friend. Perhaps the book would become a best seller. Perhaps it would even be filmed. For weeks she had hesitated. A part of her would enjoy the excitement, the fame perhaps. But another part of her worried that she would be harming Helen in some way, laying her open to the inspection of strangers and the ghouls who fed on tales of abuse, cruelty, torment. No, she couldn't do it. She had made the right decision, and yesterday she had deleted the file from her laptop. Let Helen rest in peace. Safe. Loved.

And tomorrow the house would belong to Charlotte and Adam, Alex and Emma's friends. They had seemed unperturbed by Marshbank's history.

'We don't believe in ghosts,' they said, and Charlotte had laughed. 'But it will make a good after-dinner story!'

The attic window had been fully repaired, the woodwork painted, and the walls replastered and emulsioned in pale lemon. Abi wondered if Helen would have approved.

Her mother called her. 'We should go, Abi. Are you ready?'

'Yes, just give me a minute.' She turned round slowly once more.

'Goodbye, Helen,' she whispered, although she was almost sure nothing lingered of Helen's ghost. She waited. Nothing.

'Abi!' her mother called again.

'Coming!' She turned and clattered down the stairs.

***

At eleven o'clock the next morning the new owners arrived in cavalcade. Two removal vans, two separate cars and a motor bike. Adam in the first car, the empty seats packed with the more fragile of the family's belongings; Charlotte in the second, with the couple's two daughters, Tracey and Anna; on the motor bike their son Ewan.

While Adam and Charlotte supervised the placing of furniture and equipment, the girls tore through the house, squabbling as they claimed their bedrooms. Ewan's interest was the garden, in particular the orchard where the bones of that girl had been found. What a tale he could tell his mates! He was actually living in a house where a murder had been committed! He couldn't wait to invite them here.

Two hours later, after a makeshift lunch and the departure of the removal vans, Tracey, the older of the two girls, crept up the second staircase to the attics. She too had read about the murder, had been reassured by Charlotte that there was nothing to be scared of – and she wasn't really scared, just drawn to the scene by some sort of identification with that poor girl, a girl her own age.

She would have liked to know more, but Abi, who had lived here and was now enrolled in Tracey's school, refused to disclose any details. All Tracey knew was the dead girl's name. Helen.

'Helen,' she whispered now. And louder: 'Helen?'

She waited, hearing only the sigh of a rising wind through the eaves of the house, and the crooning of pigeons on the roof.

The attic was just a room. A very small one, but perhaps large enough for Tracey to bring up her easel and her paints. Perhaps she would paint a portrait of Helen as she imagined her, a girl her own age, slim, dark haired, her skin pale for lack of sunshine. An old fashioned girl. A girl who had lived and died three quarters of a century ago.

'Helen,' she whispered again, and strained her ears for a reply. Nothing.

A call came from below. 'Tracey? Come and sort out your boxes!'

'Coming,' she called back and left the attic, closing the door behind her.

Had she stayed longer, had she called Helen again, she might have heard a reply.

I'm here. I'm still here. Stay with me.

ABOUT THE AUTHOR

Joy Wodhams has been writing as long as she can remember. She is the descendant of five generations of theatre and circus gymnasts, trapeze artists, singers, musicians and songwriters. As far as she is aware, she is the first fiction writer in the family.

At the age of seven she created her first magazine, selling it to her circle of friends for one old penny. Many years later she became a real magazine editor and then went on to sell short stories and features to national magazines. She also tutors in both Creative Writing and Art.

OTHER BOOKS BY JOY WODHAMS

Children's and YA Novels

THE MYSTERY OF CRAVEN MANOR

THE FAMILY ON PINEAPPLE ISLAND

THERE'S A LION IN MY BED!

THE BOY WHO COULD FLY

CABBAGE BOY

Fiction for Adults

ME, DINGO AND SIBELIUS

AFFAIR WITH AN ANGEL

NEVER SLEEP WITH A NEIGHBOUR!

THE RELUCTANT BRIDE

Short Story Collections

THE FLOATER

THE GIRL AT TABLE NINE

Non-Fiction

HOW TO WRITE FICTION

Excerpt from CABBAGE BOY, the strangest mutant you'll never meet

(Another of Joy's novels for teens and young adults, available on Kindle or as a paperback)

Things began to go wrong when we reached the other side of the pond, where five boys, all in their late teens, were messing about with a ball. They stopped to stare as we drew near, and then the nudges and the jeering began.

'Hey, darling, who's your girlfriend?' one shouted to Melanie.

'What's it to you?' she shouted back.

All five swaggered up to Ollie and looked him up and down. 'God, she's ugly,' said one. 'Hey, Kev, fancy a date with that?'

'You'd have to be desperate. Or blind.' Kev looked at me. 'This *your* date, kid?'

'She's my sister,' I lied, 'so watch what you say!'

'I'd leave her at home next time if I was you. She might frighten the children.' He turned to one of the others. 'What d'you think, Mick?'

Mick laughed. 'I don't think she's for real,' he said. 'I think she's their Grandad in disguise!'

The five of them, led by Kev, began to circle Ollie, taunting him.

'Look at her nose,' said Kev. 'Elephant Woman!'

'You sure she's your sister?' asked Mick. 'Look at all those wrinkles. I still reckon she's your grandad. Your *gay* grandad!'

'You shouldn't let her out in daylight – she'll give all the

261

little kiddywinks nightmares!'

'Hey, what time d'you put her back in her cage?'

Ollie stood quietly, waiting for us to move on, I suppose. I was glad he was unable to understand the insults the boys were flinging at him. But we were beginning to attract attention. The last thing we wanted. I hated the gang but what could I do?

Then Becca stepped forward, putting on her fiercest face. 'If you can't be polite, scumbags, then piss off!'

Suddenly Mick poked at Ollie's chest. And that did it. Ollie's reaction was immediate. He stepped back a pace or two, his nose came to attention and he squirted.

'Aagh! Ow! She's scalded me,' howled Mick. 'Did you see that?'

'Serve you right,' snapped Becca. If I were you I'd clear off before she does it again!'

Mick stared in disbelief at the sleeve of his shirt, drenched and steaming. 'It hurts!'

'You're lucky it was just your arm,' said Becca.

'I'm going to report this,' he yelled. 'I'm going to call the police.'

'Do that,' Becca snapped. 'What you going to say? That my kid sister spat on you after you sexually assaulted her?'

Mick gaped at her. 'Sexual assault? I never - '

'You poked her in the chest. You do that to a girl, that's sexual assault. And we're all witnesses, aren't we?' Becca nodded at me and her mates.

'Oh, leave it, Mick,' said Kev. 'They're not worth it.'

But Mick was still examining his arm and grumbling as they walked away. 'I think I'm getting blisters!'

Sometimes it's useful to have a 160lb sister who's a feminist.

Excerpt from NEVER SLEEP WITH A NEIGHBOUR!

(A light-hearted village romance)

(After Abi has mistaken Dan for an intruder and smashed a vase over his head, they meet again at a village party)

The awkward silence seemed doomed to continue until the party ended. Ali felt she had to break it.

'Look, we don't want to upset our hosts, do we? Do you think you could bring yourself to be polite to me?'

'Certainly, as long as you can refrain from hitting me on the head.'

They glared at each other. And then, despite herself, Ali felt a giggle rise into her throat, just as the corners of Dan's mouth twitched.

'This is silly!' she said.

'I agree. D'you think we could start again? I'd much rather be a friend than an enemy.'

'Me too.'

'Let me get you another drink.'

As he returned, she noticed how many people stopped him to chat. Although he had moved to the village so recently, it was clear he was already a popular figure. A prosperous looking couple had halted him now. The woman, somewhere in her forties, was absolutely stunning, with the gloss and confidence of someone who had been beautiful from birth. She was flirting outrageously with Dan, her fingers running up and down his arm, her eyes widening as she gazed up at him. Her partner (husband?) a much older man, didn't seem to mind.

'Sorry,' Dan said on his return. 'You know what it's like at these do's.'

'Who's the woman?' Ali asked.

'That's Sandy Breakspear. Her husband, Alistair, owns the Breakspear Building Supplies chain. Very prominent couple, very involved in the village. Sandy's Chairperson of the local Women's Institute.'

'You're joking!'

He laughed. 'Not at all. Sandy's a reformed character. Used to be a Bunny Girl, back in the day.'

'I can believe that. But - the WI!'

'I know. Oh, she breaks out now and again but most of the time she's the very respectable Lady of the Manor. And despite the flirting she and Alistair are very happily married. Their Ruby Wedding is coming up next year.'

Ali did some calculations. 'No! She can't possibly be old enough.'

'Ah, looks can be deceiving. Our Sandy is well into her sixties. But what about you?'

She flicked a glance at him. 'Are you asking how old I am?'

'I wouldn't dream of it!'

'I'm thirty two.'

'And already a celebrity, I hear.'

'Hardly that. My last two books have sold well, but it's still quite early in my career.'

'What do you write about?'

'Frogs.'

'Frogs? Are you some sort of zoologist?'

'Not exactly. I write for children. My hero is a frog.'

He stared at her. 'A frog,' he repeated.

She nodded. 'His name is Fergus.'

'Fergus.'

'He's a Scottish frog.'

Dan looked down at his drink, and she saw that his mouth was twitching again. 'Well,' he said at last. 'I don't know what to say.'

'In that case, don't say anything!' she snapped.

THE CIRCUS, THE BLITZ AND A TRAGIC GHOST

Last year the circus celebrated its 250th anniversary, which inspired the author to write THE BOY WHO COULD FLY.

The story is written for children (10 years upwards) but is also interesting for adults. It has a supernatural element, bringing together her own 19th century ancestor, 'Una The Human Fly', a circus aerialist tragically killed while performing at the age of 16, and Jamie, a fictional descendant of his.

It begins in Britain during WW2 with Jamie losing both parents in the Liverpool blitz and follows his subsequent life, much of it lonely and difficult, and his burning desire to learn how to fly on a trapeze.

A mix of story telling, circus lore and historical detail, parts of the book are autobiographical. Like its hero the author was born and brought up in Liverpool, and Liverpool is the setting for both THE BOY WHO COULD FLY and also one of her adult books (ME, DINGO AND SIBELIUS), in which a lowly and loveless young care worker inherits a million pounds and buys the retirement home where she works).

Printed in Great Britain
by Amazon

36518305R10152